I0557689

King Chameleon
and more
West African Folktales

Edited By Rotimi Ogunjobi

Rotimi Ogunjobi

King Chameleon and more West African Folktales

—

© 2015 Rotimi Ogunjobi

Illustrations by Ola Tejumola

ISBN: 978-978-53410-3-4

INTRODUCTION TO THE
AFRICAN NIGHT ENTERTAINMENT
SERIES

"....*picture an evening scene in a native village. The sun is nearing the western horizon, seeming to fall like a huge ball behind the distant hills, the air is cool, and a solemn stillness prevails. Even the noisy youths and girls are quiet, and the time for tom-toms, crickets, bull-frogs, and the miscellaneous instruments of man and Nature for the production of the most weird and inharmonious of sounds is not yet. In the compound—the courtyard round which are the family dwellings—the women with their picin (children) on their backs are busy with mortar and pestle making foo-foo (native food from maize). Squatting near the mud walls, naked to the waist, their cloth forming but a covering for the loins, are a number of men smoking short clay pipes and expectorating in a most insanitary manner—a perfect picture of idleness. Naked youngsters stand open-mouthed listening to the conservation of their elders, or amuse themselves at hide-and-seek, marbles, or some other native game.*

The short twilight of the tropics brings all occupations except taking to an end, and of talking there seems to be no end. Here and there someone or other lies down, covers himself entirely with his cloth, and is lost to the world.

A lantern is brought out, and unconsciously and imperceptibly it becomes the centre of dark forms, relieved now and again by rows of beautiful white teeth as the owners indulge in a hearty laugh. At times conversation lags; someone drones a monotonous tune, others smoke in quiet contemplation, while others again follow the example of the dark human mounds scattered about the compound.

Suddenly, "Comrades, listen to a story". At once the men, women, and children press round the speaker, an eager crowd, ready to hear or to tell the tales of their folk...."

-William H Barker (West African Folktales)

4

Where do stories come from?

I asked this question in the preface to a book, Ajantala and other Yoruba Folktales, which I compiled several years ago. For many African children, night time is indeed story time. Children would gathered at the foot of a storyteller, often an elderly person who would entertain them with tales filled with so much drama and passion that they did always appear real , even to listening adults.

But where did those tales come from? Most had indeed been handed down to the storyteller as a child in the same way that he had just done. Sometimes the story would have been so old that the storyteller, not being able to remember how it originally went, would add embellishment of his own crafting, and sometimes in such a proportion that an entirely different tale is consequently produced. I have myself many times, appropriated such creative license while retelling long lost stories to a children audience.

As in every part of the world, the African folktales would generally derive from the daily experience of a people, their environment, their predominant occupations, their aspirations and of course their moral rules. Indeed as an academic discipline, folklore shares methods, and insights with literature, anthropology, art, music, history, linguistics, philosophy, and mythology.

When I say a people, I must add however that the story belongs more to the teller rather than to the community. Depending therefore on the immediate disposition of the storyteller, stories can end up funny , fascinating, ridiculous or thought-provoking, . The constant purpose of the typical African folktale often remains to teach young children important lessons about wholesome values.

One would find from this African Night Entertainment series, that a folktale may be so commonly retold across the continent, that one is no more sure of the origin. As an example, there is much similarity in the story of the bad boy Ajantala, as told by Yoruba folklorist D.O Fagunwa , and the story of the bad boy Kwaku (or Koku) Baboni which existed in Akan folklore more than half a century before Ajantala . One reason for this may have been that African communities and family units used to be very migratory. Indeed, distinct towns and villages in many parts of Africa did not exist until less than three centuries ago. This reason, as well as other factors such as frequent internecine conflicts and slave-raids may have quite assisted the propagation of the folklore of a particular community. Thus, folktales which originated from a specific transient community could eventually become owned by another community, several thousands of miles away, with localized characters.

What have I added to the stories in this series ? In many cases I have tried to preserve the style of the penultimate narrator; rather than making the stories mine. The importance of this is that some folk stories are only interesting if told in a particular way ; otherwise they become so limp and like academic translations. In some cases though, it has been necessary to edit a story primarily for clarity and to simplify obscure and archaic phrases and descriptions. Typically because of the prevalent customs at the time many of these stories were originally generated, one would find instances of ritual murder and demonic manifestation casually thrown in by the narrator ; to the possible distress of the typical prudent reader of these times. In all cases however, I have strived to bring in my personal skill as a storyteller and folklorist, into compiling each priceless volume; I have attempted to give each book the entertainment value it deserves; I have tried to make each book suitable for preservation in public repositories as the current state of the journey in the storyteller's tale.

Rotimi Ogunjobi

December 2015

INTRODUCTION
TO THIS VOLUME

King Chameleon and more West African Folktales is a selection of folklore believed to have originated from West Africa and the people who live in the region. West Africa is home to several scores of tribes, languages and dialects.

Even though, tribal cords are quite strong and languages may differ markedly even between two communities a few hundred miles apart, it is usual to find similarities between the local folktales , and in some cases only the names of the central characters would make one version of a tale to be different from another .

Most of the stories in this volume were gleaned from areas within the countries now known as Ghana and Togo. However, the stories are commonly retold in several forms all over the West Africa region.

Acknowledgement for some stories in this collection:

West African Folk Tales

By William H. Barker and Cecilia Sinclair

George G. Harrap & Company (1917)

—

CONTENTS

AM BOOK AND TEAM PUBLISHING LIMITED

AM Book and Team Publishing Limited
1 Olanipekun Street , Ososami Road, Ibadan
Telephone: 08098744910
mail@ambookpublishing.com
www.ambookpublishing.com

Rotimi Ogunjobi

HOW WISDOM CAME
TO THE WORLD

THERE once lived, in Fanti-land, a man named Father Anansi. He possessed all the wisdom in the world. People came to him daily for advice and help.

One day the men of the country were unfortunate enough to offend Father Anansi, who immediately resolved to punish them. After much thought he decided that the severest penalty he could inflict would be to hide all his wisdom from them. He set to work at once to gather again all that he had already given. When he had succeeded, as he thought, in collecting it, he placed all in one great pot. This he carefully sealed, and determined to put it in a spot where no human being could reach it.

Now, Father Anansi had a son, whose name was Kwaku Tsin. This boy began to suspect his father of some secret plan, so he made up his mind to watch carefully. Next day he saw his father quietly slip out of the house, with his precious pot hung round his neck. Kwaku Tsin followed. Father Anansi went through the forest till he had left the village far behind. Then, selecting the highest and most inaccessible-looking tree, he began to climb. The heavy pot, hanging

13

in front of him, made his ascent almost impossible. Again and again he tried to reach the top of the tree, where he intended to hang the pot. There, he thought, Wisdom would indeed be beyond the reach of everyone but himself. He was unable, however, to carry out his desire. At each trial the pot swung in his way.

For sometime Kwaku Tsin watched his father's vain attempts. At last, unable to contain himself any longer, he cried out: "Father, why do you not hang the pot on your back? Then you could easily climb the tree".

Father Anansi turned and said: "I thought I had the entire world's wisdom in this pot. But I find you possess more than I do. All my wisdom was insufficient to show me what to do, yet you have been able to tell me". In his anger he threw the pot down. It struck on a great rock and broke. The wisdom contained in it escaped and spread throughout the world.

ANANSI AND NOTHING

NEAR Anansi's miserable little hut there was a fine palace where lived a very rich man called Nothing. Nothing and Anansi proposed, one day, to go to the neighboring town to get some wives. Accordingly, they set off together.

Nothing, being a rich man, wore a very fine velvet cloth, while Anansi had s ragged cotton one. While they were on their way Anansi persuaded nothing to change clothes for a little while, promising to give back the fine velvet before they reached the town. He delayed doing this, however, first on one pretext, then on another—till they arrived at their destination.

Anansi, being dressed in such a fine garment, found no difficulty in getting as many wives as he wished. Poor Nothing, with his ragged and miserable cloth, was treated with great contempt. At first he could not get even one wife. At last, however, a woman took pity on him and gave him her daughter. The poor girl was laughed at very heartily by Anansi's wives for choosing such a beggar as nothing appeared to be. She wisely took no notice of their scorn.

The party set off for home. When they reached the cross-roads leading to their respective houses the women were astonished.

15

The road leading to Anansi's house was only half cleared. The one which led to nothing's place was, of course, wide and well made. Not only so, but his servants had strewn it with beautiful skins and carpets, in preparation for his return. Servants were there, awaiting him, with fine clothes for himself and his wife. No one was waiting for Anansi.

Nothing's wife was queen over the whole district and had everything her heart could not even get proper food; they had to live on unripe bananas with peppers. The wife of nothing heard of her friends' miserable state and invited them to a great feast in her palace. They came, and were so pleased with all they saw that they agreed to stay there. Accordingly, they refused to come back to Anansi's hut.

He was very angry, and tried in many ways to kill Nothing, but without success. Finally, however, he persuaded some rat friends to dig a deep tunnel in front of Nothing's door. When the hole was finished Anansi lined it with knives and broken bottles. He then smeared the steps of the palace with *okro* to make them very slippery, and withdrew to a little distance.

When he thought nothing's household was safely in bed and asleep, he called to nothing to come out to the courtyard and see something. Nothing's wife, however, dissuaded him from going.

Anansi tried again and again, and each time she made her husband not to listen. At last nothing determined to go and see this thing. As he placed his foot on the first step, of course he slipped, and down he fell into the hole. The noise alarmed the household. Lights were fetched and Nothing was found in the ditch, so much wounded by the knives that he soon died. His wife was terribly grieved at his untimely death. She boiled many yams, mashed them, and took a great dishful of them round the district. To every child she met she gave some, so that the child might help her to cry for her husband. This is why, if you find a child crying and ask the cause, you will often be told he is "crying for nothing".

THUNDER AND ANANSI

THERE had been a long and severe famine in the land where Anansi lived. He had been quite unable to obtain food for his poor wife and family. One day, gazing desperately out to sea, he saw, rising from the midst of the water, a tiny island with a tall palm-tree upon it. He determined to reach this tree—if any means proved possible—and climb it, in the hope of finding a few nuts to reward him. How to get there was the difficulty.

This, however, solved itself when he reached the beach, for there lay the means to his hand, in the shape of an old broken boat. It certainly did not look very strong, but Anansi decided to try it.

His first six attempts were unsuccessful—a great wave dashed him back on the beach each time he tried to put off. He was persevering, however, and at the seventh trial was successful in getting away. He steered the battered old boat as best he could, and at length reached the palm-tree of his desire. Having tied the boat to the trunk of thee tree—which grew almost straight out of the water—he climbed toward the nuts. Plucking all he could reach, he dropped them, one by one, down to the boat. To his dismay, everyone missed the boat and fell; instead, into the water until only the last one remained. This he aimed even more carefully than the others, but it also fell into the water and disappeared from his hungry eyes. He had not tasted even one and now all were gone.

He could not bear the thought of going home empty-handed, so, in his despair, he threw himself into the water, too. To his complete astonishment, instead of being drowned, he found himself standing on the sea-bottom in front of a pretty little cottage. From the latter came an old man, who asked Anansi what he wanted so badly that he had come to Thunder's cottage to seek it. Anansi told his tale of woe, and Thunder showed himself most sympathetic.

He went into the cottage and fetched a fine cooking-pot, which he presented to Anansi—telling him that he need never be hungry again. The pot would always supply enough food for himself and his family. Anansi was most grateful, and left Thunder with many thanks.

Being anxious to test the pot at once, Anansi only waited till he was again seated in the old boat to say "pot, pot what you used to do for your master do now for me". Immediately good food of all sorts appeared. Anansi ate a hearty meal, which he very much enjoyed.

On reaching land again, his first thought was to run home and give all his family a good meal from his wonderful pot. A selfish, greedy fear prevented him. "What if I should use up all the magic of the pot on them, and have nothing more left for myself! Better keep the pot a secret—then I can enjoy a meal when I want one". So, his mind full of this thought, he did the pot.

He reached home, pretending to be utterly worn out with fatigue and hunger. There was not a grain of food to be anywhere. His wife and poor children were weak with want of it, but selfish Anansi took no notice of that. He congratulated himself at the thought of his magic pot, now safely hidden in his room. There he retired from time to time when he felt hungry, and enjoyed a good meal. His family got thinner and thinner, but he grew plumber and plumber. They began suspect some secret, and determined to find it out. His eldest son, Kwaku Tsin, had the power of changing himself into any shape he chose; so he took the form of a tiny fly, and accompanied his father everywhere. At last, Anansi, feeling hungry, entered his room and closed the door. Next he took the pot, and had a fine meal. Having replaced the pot in its hiding-place, he went out, on the pretence of looking for food.

As soon as he was safely out of sight, Kwaku Tsin fetched out the pot and called all his hungry family to come at once. They had as good a meal as their father had. When they finished, Mrs. Anansi—to punish her husband—said she would take the pot down to the village and give everybody a meal. This she did—but alas! In working to prepare so much food at one time, the pot grew too hot and melted away. What was to be done now? Anansi would be so angry! His wife forbade everyone to mention the pot.

Anansi returned, ready for his supper, and, as usual, went into his room, carefully shutting the door. He went to the hiding-place—it was empty! He looked around in consternation. No pot was to be seen anywhere. Someone must be culprits; he would find a means to punish them.

Saying nothing to anyone about the matter, he waited till morning. As soon as it was light started off towards the shore, where the old boat lay. Getting into the boat, it started of its own accord and glided swiftly over the water—straight for the palm tree. Arrived there, Anansi attached the boat as before and climbed the tree. This time, unlike the last, the nuts almost fell into his hands. When he aimed them at the boat they fell easily into it—not one, as before, dropping into the water. He deliberately took them and threw them overboard, immediately jumping after them. As before, he found himself in front of Thunder's cottage, with Thunder waiting to hear his tale. This he told, the old man showing the same sympathy as he had previously done.

This time, however, he presented Anansi with a fine stick and bade him good-bye. Anansi could scarcely wait till he got into the boat—so anxious was he to try the magic properties of his new gift. "Stick, Stick", he said, "What you used to do for your master do for me also". The stick began to beat him so severely that, in a few minutes, he was obliged to jump into the water and swim ashore, leaving boat and stick to drift away where they pleased. Then he returned sorrowfully homeward, bemoaning his many bruises and wishing he had acted more wisely from the beginning.

WHY THE LIZARD
CONTINUALLY NODS HIS HEAD

IN a town not very far from Anansi's home lived a great king. This king had three beautiful daughters, whose names were kept a secret from everybody except their own family. One day their father made a proclamation that his three daughters would be given as wives to any man who could find out their names. Anansi made up his mind to do so.

He first brought a large jar of honey, and set off for the bathing-place of the king's daughters. Arrived there, he climbed to the top of a tree on which grew some very fine fruit. He picked some of this fruit and poured honey over it. When he saw the princesses approaching he dropped the fruit on the ground and waited. The girls thought the fruit dropped of its own accord, and one of them ran forward to pick it up. When she tasted it, she called out to her sisters by name to exclaim on its sweetness. Anansi dropped another, which the second princess picked up—she, in her turn, calling out the names of the other two. In this fashion Anansi found out all the names.

As soon as the princesses had gone Anansi came down from the tree and hurried into the town. He went to all the great men and summoned them to a meeting at the king's palace on tomorrow.

He then visited his friend the Lizard, to get him to act as herald at the Court next day. He told Lizard the three names, and the latter was to sound them through his trumpet when the time came.

Early next morning the King and his Court were assembled as usual. All the great men of the town appeared, as Anansi had requested. Anansi stated his business, reminding the King of his promise to give his three daughters to the man who had found out their names. The King demanded to hear the latter, whereupon Lizard sounded them on his trumpet.

The King and courtiers were much surprised. His Majesty, however, could not break the promise he had made of giving his daughters to the man who named them. He accordingly gave them to Mr. Lizard. Anansi was very angry, and explained that he had told the names to Lizard, so that he ought to get at least two of the girls, while Lizard could have the third. The king refused. Anansi then begged hard for even one, but that was also refused. He went home in a very bad temper, declaring that he would be revenged on Lizard for stealing his wives away.

He thought over the matter very carefully, but could not find a way of punishing Lizard. At last, however, he had an idea.

He went to the king and explained that he was setting off next morning on a long journey. He wished to start very early, and so begged the King's help. The King had a fine cock, which always crowed at daybreak to wake the King if he wished to get up early. Anansi begged that the King would command the cock to crow next morning, that Anansi might be sure of getting off in time. This the King readily promised.

As soon as night fell Anansi went by a back way to the cock's sleeping-place, seized the bird quickly, and killed it. He then carried it to Lizard's house, where all were in bed. There he quietly cooked the cock, placed the feathers under Lizard's bed, and put some of the flesh on a dish close to Lizard's hand. The wicked Anansi then took some boiling water and poured it into poor Lizard's mouth, thus making him dumb.

When morning came, Anansi went to the king and reproached him for not letting the cock crow. The king was much surprised to hear that it had not obeyed his commands.

He sent one of his servants to find and bring the cock to him, but, of course, the servant returned empty-handed. The King then ordered them to find the thief. No trace of him could be found anywhere. Anansi then cunningly said to the King: "I know Lizard is a rogue, because he stole my three wives from me. Perhaps he is the thief". Accordingly, the men went to search Lizard's house.

There, of course, they found the remnants of the cock, cooked ready to eat, and his feathers under the bed. They questioned Lizard, but the poor animal was unable to reply. He could only move his head up and down helplessly. They thought he was refusing to speak, so dragged him before the King. To the king's questions he could only return the same answer, and his Majesty got very angry. He did not know that Anansi had made the poor animal dumb. Lizard tried very hard to speak, but in vain.

He was accordingly judged guilty of theft, and as a punishment his wives were taken away from him and given to Anansi.

Since then lizards have always had a way of moving their heads helplessly backward and forward, as if saying, "How can anyone be so foolish as to trust Anansi"?

TIT FOR TAT

THERE had been a great famine in the land for many months. Meat had become so scarce that only the rich chiefs had money enough to buy it. The poor people were starving. Anansi and his family were in a miserable state.

One day, Anansi's eldest son—Kwaku Tsin—to his great joy, discovered a place in the forest where there were still many animals. Knowing his father's wicked ways, Kwaku told him nothing of the matter. Anansi, however, speedily discovered that Kwaku was returning loaded, day after day, to the village. There he was able to sell the meat at a good price to the hungry villagers. Anansi immediately wanted to know the secret—but his son wisely refused to tell him. The old man determined to find out by a trick.

Slipping into his son's room one night, when he was fast asleep, he cut a tiny hole in the corner of the bag which Kwaku always carried into the forest. Anansi then put a quantity of ashes into the bag and replaced it where he had found it.

Next morning, as Kwaku set out for the forest, he threw the bag, as usual, over his shoulder. Unknown to him, at each step, the ashes were sprinkled on the ground. Consequently, when Anansi set out an hour later he was easily able to follow his son by means of the trail of ashes. He, too, arrived at the animals' home in the forest, and found Kwaku there before him. He immediately drove his son away, saying that, by the law of the land, the place belonged to him. Kwaku saw how he had been tricked, and determined to have the meat back.

He accordingly went home—made a tiny image and hung little bells round its neck. He then tied a long thread to its head and returned toward the hunting-place.

When about half-way there, he hung the image to a branch of a tree in the path, and hid himself in the bushes near by—holding the other end of the thread in his hand.

The greedy father, in the meantime, had killed as many animals as he could find, being determined to become rich as speedily as possible. He then skinned them and prepared the flesh—to carry it to the neighboring villages to sell. Taking the first load, he set off for his own village. Half-way there, he came to the place where the image hung in the way. Thinking this was one of the gods, he stopped. As he approached, the image began to shake its head vigorously at him. He felt that this meant that the gods were angry. To please them, he said to the image, "May I give you a little of this meat?" Again the image shook its head. "May I give you half of this meat?" he then inquired. The head shook once more. "Do you want the whole of this meat?" he shouted fiercely. This time the head nodded, as if the image were well pleased. "I will *not* give you all my meat," Anansi cried. At this the image shook in every limb as if in a terrible temper. Anansi was so frightened that back, "To-morrow I shall go to Ekubon—you will not be able to take my meat from me there, you thief".

But Kwaku had heard where his father intended to go next day—and set the image in his path as before. Again Anansi was obliged to leave his whole load—and again he called out the name of the place where he would go the following day.

The same thing occurred, day after day, till all the animals in the wood were killed. By this time, Kwaku Tsin had become very rich—but his father Anansi was still very poor. He was obliged to go to Kwaku's house every day for food.

When the famine was over, Kwaku gave a great feast and invited the entire village. While all were gathered together, Kwaku told the story of his father's cunning and how it had been overcome. This caused great merriment among the villagers. Anansi was so ashamed that he readily promised Kwaku to refrain from his evil tricks for the future. This promise, however, he did not long keep.

WHY WHITE ANTS
ALWAYS DESTROY HOUSES

THERE came once such a terrible famine in the land that a grain corn was worth far more than its weight in gold. A hungry spider was wandering through the forest looking for food. To his great joy he found a dead antelope.

Knowing that he would not be allowed to reach home in safety with it, he wrapped it up very carefully in a long mat and bound it securely.

Placing it on his head, he started for home. As he went, he wept bitterly, telling everyone that this was his dead grandfather's body. Everyone he met sympathized heartily with him.

On his way he met the wolf and the leopard. These two wise animals suspected that this was one of Spider's tricks. They knew that he was not to be trusted. Walking on a little way, they discussed what they could do to find out what was in the bundle.

They agreed to take a short cut across the country to a tree which they knew Cousin Spider must pass. When they reached this tree they hid themselves very carefully behind it and waited for him.

As he passed the place they shook the tree and uttered frightful noises. This so frightened Mr. Spider that he dropped his load and ran away.

The two gentlemen opened the bundle and, to their great joy, discovered the flesh of the antelope in it. They carried it off to their own home and began to prepare supper.

When Mr. Spider recovered from his fear he began to wonder who could have been at the tree to make the noises. He decided that his enemies must be Wolf and Leopard. He made up his mind he would get his meat back from them.

He took a small lizard and filed his teeth to fine, sharp points. He then sent him to spy upon the wolf and leopard—by begging fire from them. He was to get the fire and quench it as soon as he left their cottage. He could then return and ask a second time. If they asked him questions, he must smile and show his teeth.

The lizard did as he was told, and everything turned out just as Spider had expected. Wolf and Leopard eagerly asked the lizard where he had his teeth filed so beautifully. He replied that "Filling Spider" had done it for him.

Wolf and Leopard discussed the matter and decided to have their teeth filed in the same way. They could then easily break the bones of their food.

Accordingly, they went to the house of the disguised spider and asked him to make their teeth like Lizard's. Spider agreed, but said that, to do it properly, he would first have to hang them on a tree. They made no objection to this.

When he had them safely hung, Spider and his family came and mocked them. Spider then went to their cottage and brought away the body of the antelope. The whole village was invited to the feast, which was held in front of the two poor animals on the tree. During this festival every one made fun of the wolf and leopard.

Next morning White Ant and his children passed the place on their way to some friends. Mr. Leopard begged them to set him and his friend free. White Ant and his family set to work, destroyed the tree and set them at liberty. Leopard and Wolf promised the ants that on their return they would spread a feast for them.

Unfortunately, spider heard the invitation and made up his mind to benefit by it. On the third day (which was the very time set by the wolf and leopard) Spider dressed up his children like an ants. They set out, singing the ants' chorus, in order to deceive Leopard.

Wolf and Leopard welcomed them heartily and spread a splendid feast for them, which the spiders thoroughly enjoyed.

Soon after their departure the real ants arrived. The two hosts, thinking these must be spider and his family, poured boiling water over them and killed them all expect the father.

White Ant, on reaching home again, in great anger, vowed that he would never again help anyone. He would take every opportunity to destroy houses. From that day to this white ants have been a perfect pest to man.

THE SQUIRREL
AND THE SPIDER

A HARD-WORKING squirrel had, after much labor, succeeded in cultivating a very fine farm. Being a skillful climber of trees, he had not troubled to make a roadway into his farm. He used to reach it by the trees.

One day, when his harvests were very nearly ripe, it happened that Spider went out hunting in that neighborhood. During his travels, he arrived at Squirrel's farm. Greatly pleased at the appearance on the fields, he sought for the roadway to it. Finding none, he returned home and told his family all about the matter. The very next day they all set out for this fine place, and set to work immediately to make a road. When this was completed Spider—who was very cunning—threw pieces of earthenware pot along the pathway. This he did to make believe that his children had dropped them while working to prepare the farm.

Then he and his family began to cut down and carry away such of the corn as was ripe. Squirrel noticed that his fields were being robbed, but could not at first find the thief. He determined to watch. Sure enough Spider soon reappeared to steal more of the

35

harvest. Squirrel demanded to know what right he had on these fields. Spider immediately asked him the same question. "They are my fields," said Squirrel. "Oh, no! They are mine," retorted Spider. "I dug them and sowed them and planted them," said poor squirrel. "Then where is your roadway to them?" said crafty Spider. "I need no roadway. I come by the trees," was Squirrel's reply. Needless to say, spider laughed such an answer to scorn, and continued to use the farm as his own.

Squirrel appealed to the law, but the court decided that no one had ever had a farm without a road leading to it; therefore the fields must be spiders.

In great glee Spider and his family prepared to cut down all the harvest that remained. When it was cut they tied in it great bundles and set off to the nearest market-place to sell it. When they were about half-way there, a terrible storm came on. They were obliged to put down their burdens by the roadside and run for shelter. When the storm had passed they returned to pick up their loads.

As they approached the spot they found a great, black crow there, with his broad wings outspread to keep the bundles dry. Spider went to him and very politely thanked him for so kindly taking care of their property. "Your property!" replied Father Crow. "Who ever heard of anyone leaving bundles of corn by the roadside? Nonsense! These loads are mine". So saying, he picked them up and went off with them, leaving Spider and his children to return home sorrowful and empty-handed. Their thieving ways had brought them little profit.

WHY ANTS
CARRY HUGE LOADS

KWAKU ANANSI and Kwaku Tsin—his son—were both very clever farmers. Generally they succeeded in getting fine harvests from each of their farms. One year, however, they were very unfortunate. They had shown their seeds as usual, but no rain had fallen for more than a month after and it looked as if the seeds would be unable to sprout.

Kwaku Tsin was walking sadly through his fields one day looking at the bare, dry ground, and wondering what he and his family would do for food, if they were unable to get any harvest. To his surprise he saw a tiny dwarf seated by the roadside. The little hunchback asked the reason of his sadness, and Kwaku Tsin told him. The dwarf promised to help him by bringing rain on the farm. He bade Kwaku fetch two small sticks and tap him lightly on the hump, while he sung:

"O water, go up, O water, go up,

And let rain fall, and let rain fall."

To Kwaku's great joy rain immediately began to fall, and continued till the ground was thoroughly well soaked. In the days following the seeds germinated, and the crops began to promise well.

Anansi soon heard how well Kwaku's crops were growing—whilst his own were still bare and hard. He went straightway to his son and demanded to know the reason. Kwaku Tsin, being an honest fellow, at once told him what had happened.

Anansi quickly made up his mind to get his farm watered in the same way, and accordingly set out toward it. As he went, he cut two big, strong sticks, thinking, "My son made the dwarf work with little sticks. I will make him do twice as much with my big ones." He carefully hid the big sticks, however, when he saw the dwarf coming toward him. As before, the hunchback asked what the trouble was, and Anansi told him. "Take two small sticks, and beat me lightly on the hump," said the dwarf. "I will get rain for you".

But Anansi took his big sticks and beat so hard that the dwarf fell down dead. The greedy fellow was now thoroughly frightened, for he knew that the dwarf was jester to the King of the country, and a very great favourite of his. He wondered how he could fix the blame on someone else. He picked up the dwarf's dead body and carried it to a kola-tree. There he laid it on one of the top branches and sat down under the tree to watch.

By and by Kwaku Tsin came along to see if his father had succeeded in getting rain for his crops. Did you not see the dwarf, father?" he asked, as he saw the old man sitting alone. "Oh, yes!" replied Anansi; "but he has climbed this tree to pick kola. I am now waiting for him." "I will go up and fetch him", said the young man— and immediately began to climb. As soon as his head touched the body the latter, of course, fell to the ground. "Oh! What have you done, you wicked fellow?" cried his father. "You have killed the King's jester!" "That is all right", quietly replied the son (who saw that this was one of Anansi's tricks). "The king is very angry with him, and has promised a bag of money to anyone who would kill him. I will now and go and get the reward". "No! No! No!" shouted Anansi. "The reward is mine. I killed him with two big sticks. *I* will take him to the king". "Very well!" was the son's reply. "As you killed him, you may take him."

Off set Anansi, quite pleased with the prospect of getting a reward. He reached the King's court, only to find the king very angry at the death of his favorite. The body of the jester was shut up in a great box and Anansi was condemned—as a punishment—to carry it on his head for ever. The king enchanted the box so that it could never be set down on the ground. The only way in which Anansi could ever get rid of it was by getting some other man to put it on his head. This, of course, no one was willing to do.

At last, one day, when Anansi was almost worn out with his heavy burden, he met the ant. "Will you hold this box for me while I go to market and buy some things I need badly?" said Anansi to Mr. Ant. "I know your tricks, Anansi," replied Ant. "You want to be rid of it." "Oh, no, indeed, Mr. Ant," protested Anansi. "Indeed I will come back for it, I promise."

Mr. Ant, who was an honest fellow, and always kept his own promise, believed him. He took the box on his head, and Anansi hurried off. Needless to say, the sly fellow had not the least intention of keeping his word. Mr. Ant waited in vain for his return—and was obliged to wander all the rest of his life with the box on his head. That is the reason we so often see ants carrying a great bundles as they hurry along.

WHY SPIDERS LIVE IN THE CORNERS OF THE CEILING

EGYA ANANSI was a very skilful farmer. He, with his wife and son, set to work one year to prepare a farm, much larger than any they had previously worked. They planted in it yams, maize, and beans—and were rewarded by a very rich crop. Their harvest was quite ten times greater than any they had ever had before. Egya Anansi was very well pleased when he saw his wealth of corn and beans.

He was, however, an exceedingly selfish and greedy man, who never liked to share anything—even with his own life and son. When he saw that the crops were quite ripe, he thought of a plan whereby he alone would profit by them. He called his wife and son to him and spoke thus: "We have all three worked exceedingly hard to prepare these fields. They have well repaid us. We will now gather in the harvest and pack it away in our barns. When that is done, we shall be in need of a rest. I propose that you and our son should go back to our home in the village and remain there at your ease for two or three weeks. I have to go to the coast on very urgent business. When I return we will all come to the farm and enjoy our well-earned feast."

Anansi's wife and son thought this a very good, sensible plan, and at once agreed to it. They went straight back to their village, leaving the cunning husband to start on his journey. Needless to say he had not the slightest intention of so doing.

Instead, he built himself a very comfortable hut near the farm—supplied it with all manner of cooking utensils, gathered in a large store of the corn and vegetables from the barn, and prepared for a solitary feast. This went on for a fortnight. By that time Anansi's son began to think it was time for him to go and weed the farm, lest the weeds should grow too high. He accordingly went there and worked several hours on it. While passing the barn, he happened to look in. Great was his surprise to see that more than half of their magnificent harvest had gone. He was greatly disturbed, thinking robbers had been at work, and wondered how he could prevent further mischief.

Returning to the village, he told the people there what had happened, and they helped to make a rubber-man. When evening came they carried the sticky figure to the farm, and placed it in the midst of the fields, to frighten away thieves. Some of the young men remained with Anansi's son to watch in one of the barns.

When all was dark, Egya Anansi (quite unaware of what had happened) came, as usual, out of his hiding-place to fetch more food. On his way to the barn he saw in front of him the figure of a man, and at first felt very frightened. Finding that the man did not move, however, he gained confidence and went up to him. "What do you want here?" said he. There was no answer. He repeated his question with the same result. Anansi then became very angry and dealt the figure a blow on the cheek with his right hand. Of course, his hand stuck fast to the rubber. "How dare you hold my hand?" he exclaimed. "Let me go at once or I shall hit you again." He then hit the figure with his left hand, which also stuck. He tried to disengage himself by pushing against it with his knees and body, until, finally, knees, body, hands, and head were all firmly attached to the rubber-man. There Egya Anansi had to stay till daybreak, when his son came out with the other villagers to catch the robber. They were astonished to find that the evil-doer was Anansi himself. He, on the other hand, was so ashamed to be caught in the act of greediness that he changed into a spider and took refuge in a dark corner of the ceiling lest anyone should see him. Since then spiders have always been found in dark, dusty corners, where people are not likely to notice them.

ANANSI THE BLIND FISHERMAN

ANANSI, in his old age, became a fisherman. Very soon after that his sight began to fail. Finally, he grew quite blind. However, still being very strong, he continued his fishing – with the help of two men. The latter were exceedingly kind to him, and aided him in every possible way. They led him, each morning, to the beach and into the canoe. They told him where to spread his net and when to pull it in. When they returned to land they told him just where and when to step out, so that he did not even get wet.

Day after day this went on, but Anansi – insisted of being in the least grateful to them – behaved very badly. When they told him where to spread his net, he would reply sharply, "I know. I was just about to put it there." When they were directing him to get out of the boat, he would say, "Oh, I know perfectly well we are at the beach. I was just getting ready to step out."

This went on for a long time, Anansi getting ruder and ruder to his helpers every day, until they could bear his treatment no longer. They determined when opportunity offered to punish him for his ingratitude.

The next day, as usual, he came with them to the beach. When they had got the canoe ready, they bade him step in. "Do you think 1 am a fool?" said he. "I know the canoe is there." They made no answer, but got in and patiently pulled toward the fishing-place. When they told him where to spread his net, he replied with so much abuse that they determined, there and then, to punish him.

By this time the canoe was full of fish, so they turned to row home. When had gone a little way they stopped and said to him, "Here we are at the beach." He promptly told them that were very foolish – to tell him a thing he knew so well. He added many rude and insulting remarks, which made them thoroughly angry. He then jumped proudly out, expecting to land on the beach. To his great astonishment he found himself sinking in deep water. The two men rowed quickly away, leaving him to struggle.

Like all the men of that country he was a good swimmer, but, of course, being blind, he was unable to see where the land lay. So he swam until he was completely tired out – and was drowned.

ADZO AND HER MOTHER

THERE once lived a woman who had one great desire. She longed to have a daughter – but alas! She was childless. She could never feel happy, because of this unfulfilled wish. Even in the midst of a feast the thought would be in her mind – "Ah! If only I had a daughter to share this with me."

One day she was gathering yams in the field, and it chanced that she pulled out one which was very straight and well shaped. "Ah!" she thought to herself, "if only this fine yam were a daughter, how happy I should be." To her astonishment the yam answered. If I were to become your daughter, would you promise never to reproach me with having been a yam?" She eagerly gave her promise, and at once the yam changed into a beautiful, well-made girl. The woman was overjoyed and was very kind to the girl. She named her Adzo. The latter was exceedingly useful to her mother. She would make the bread, gather the yams, and sell them at the market-place.

She had been detained, one day, longer than usual. Her mother became impatient at her non-appearance and angrily said,

"Where can Adzo be? She does not deserve that beautiful name. She is only a yam."

A bird singing nearby heard the mother's words and immediately flew off to the tree under which Adzo sat. There he began to sing:

"Adzo! Adzo!

Your mother is unkind – she says you are only a yam,

You do not deserve your name!

Adzo! Adzo!"

The girl heard him and returned home weeping. When the woman saw her she said, "My daughter, my daughter! What is the matter?" Adzo replied:

"Oh, my mother! My mother!

You have reproached me with being a yam.

You said I did not deserve my name.

Oh, my mother! My mother!"

With these words she made her way toward the yam-field. Her mother, filled with fear, followed her, wailing.

"Nay Adzo! Adzo!

Do not believe it – do not believe it.

You are my daughter, my dear daughter

Adzo!"

But she was too late. Her daughter, still singing her sad little song, quickly changed back into a yam. When the woman arrived at the field there lay the yam on the ground, and nothing she could do or say would give her back the daughter she had desired so earnestly and treated so inconsiderately.

THE GRINDING-STONE
THAT GROUND FLOUR BY ITSELF

THERE had been another great famine throughout the land. The villagers looked thin and pale for lack of food. Only one family appeared healthy and well. This was the household of Anansi's cousin.

Anansi was unable to understand this, and felt sure his cousin was getting food in some way. The greedy fellow determined to find out the secret.

What had happened was this: Spider's cousin, while hunting one morning, had discovered a wonderful stone. The stone lay on the grass in the forest and ground flour of its own accord. Nearby ran a stream of honey. Kofi was delighted. He sat down and had a good meal. Not being a greedy man, he took away with him only enough for his family's needs.

Each morning he returned to the stone and got sufficient food for that day. In this manner he and his family kept well and plump, while the surroundings villagers were starved and miserable-looking.

Anansi gave him no peace till he promised to show him the stone. This he was most unwilling to do – knowing his cousin's wicked ways. He felt sure that when Anansi saw the stone he would not be content to take only what he needed. However, Anansi troubled him so much with questions that at last he promised. He told Anansi that they would start next morning, as soon as the women set about their work. Anansi was too impatient to wait. In the middle of the night he bade his children get up and make a noise with the pots as if they were the women at work. Spider at once ran and wakened his cousin, saying, "Quick! It is time to start." His cousin, however, saw he had been tricked, and went back to bed again, saying he would not start till the women were sweeping. No sooner was he asleep again than Spider made his children take brooms and begin to sweep very noisily. He roused Kofi once more, saying, "It is time we had started." Once more his cousin refused to set off – saying it was only another trick of Spider's he again returned to bed and to sleep. This time Spider slipped into his cousin's room and cut a hole in the bottom of his bag, which he then filled with ashes. After that he went off and left Kofi in peace.

When morning came the cousin awoke. Seeing no sign of Spider he very gladly set off alone to the forest, thinking he had rid of tiresome fellow. He was no sooner seated by the stone, however, that Anansi appeared, having followed him by the trail of ashes.

"Aha!" cried he. "Here is plenty of food for all. No more need to starve." "Hush," said his cousin. "You must not shout here. The place is too wonderful. Sit down quietly and eat."

They had a good meal and Kofi prepared to return home with enough for his family. "No, no!" cried Anansi. "I am going to take the stone." In vain did his friend try to overcome his greed? Anansi insisted on putting the stone of his head, and setting out for the village.

"Spider, spider, put me down," said stone.

"The pig came and drank and went away.

The antelope came and fed and went away:

Spider, spider, put me down.

Spider, however, refused to listen. He carried the stone from village to village selling flour, until his bag was full of money. He then set out for home.

Having reached his hut and feeling very tired he prepared to put the stone down. But the stone refused to be move from his head. It stuck fast there, and no efforts could displace it. The weight of it very soon grew too much for Anansi, and ground him down into small pieces, which were completely covered over by the stone. That is why we often find tiny spiders gathered together under large stones.

MORNING SUNRISE

A MAN in one of the villages had a very beautiful daughter. She was so lovely that people called her "Morning Sunrise." Every young man who saw her wanted to marry her. Three, in particular, were very anxious to have her for their wife. Her father found it difficult to decide among them. He determined to find out by a trick which of the three was most worthy of her.

He bade her lie down on her bed as if she were dead. He then sent the report of her death to each of the tree lovers, asking them to come and help him with her funeral.

The messenger came first to Wise Man. When he heard the message, he exclaimed, "What can this man mean? The girl is not my wife. I certainly will not pay any money for her funeral."

The messenger came next to the second man. His name was Wit. The latter at once said, "Oh dear, no! I shall not pay any money for her funeral expenses. Her father did not even let me know she was ill." So he refused to go.

Thinker, the third young man – when he received the message – at once got ready to start.

"Certainly I must go and mourn for Morning Sunrise," he said. "Had she lived, surely she would have been my wife." So he took money with him and set out for her home.

When he reached it her father called out, "Morning Sunrise, Morning Sunrise. Come here. This is your true husband."

That very day the betrothal took place, and soon after the wedding followed. Thinker and his beautiful wife lived very happily together.

WHY THE CAPTURED SEA-TURTLE BEATS ITS BREAST WITH ITS FORE-LEGS

MANY centuries ago, the people of this earth were much troubled by floods. The sea used at times to overflow its usual boundaries and sweep across the low, sandy stretches of land which bordered it. Time and again this happened, many lives being lost at each flood. Mankind was very troubled to find an escape from this oft-repeated disaster. He could think of no way of avoiding it.

Fortunately for him the wise turtle came to his help. "Take my advice," said she, "and plant rows of palms along the sea-coast. They will bind the sand together and keep it from being washed so easily away." He did so, with great success. The roots of the palms kept the sand firmly in its place. When the time came again for the sea to overflow, it washed just to the line of trees and came no farther.

Thus many lives were saved annually by the kind forethought of the turtle.

In return – one would think – mankind would protect and cherish this poor animal. But no! Each time a turtle comes to the seashore to lay her eggs among the sand, she is caught and killed for the sake of her flesh. It is the thought of the ingratitude of mankind to her, which makes her, beat her breast with her fore-legs when she is caught. She seems to be saying, "Ah! This is all the return I get for my kindness to you."

HOW BEASTS AND SERPENTS
FIRST CAME INTO THE WORLD

THE famine had lasted nearly three years. Kwaku Tsin, being very hungry, looked daily in the forest in the hope of finding food. One day he was fortunate enough to discover three palm-kernels lying on the ground. He picked up two stones with which to crack them. The first nut, however, slipped when he hit it, and fell into a hole behind him. The same thing happened to the second and to the third. Very much annoyed at his loss, Kwaku determined to go down the hole to see if he could find his lost nuts.

To his surprise, however, he discovered that this hole was really the entrance to a town, of which he had never before even heard. When he reached it he found absolute silence everywhere. He called out, "Is there nobody in this town?" and presently heard a voice in answer. He went in its direction and found an old woman sitting in one of the houses. She demanded the reason of his appearance – which he readily gave.

The old woman was very kind and sympathetic, and promised to help him. "You must do exactly as I tell you," said she. "Go into the garden and listen attentively. You will hear the yams speak. Pass by any yam that says, 'Dig me out, dig me out!' But take the one that says, 'Do not dig me out!' Then bring it to me."

When he brought it, she directed him to remove the peel from the yam and throw the latter away. He was then boiled the rind, and, while boiling, it would become yam. It did actually do so, and they sat down to eat some of it. Before beginning their meal the old woman requested Kwaku not to look at her while she ate. Being very polite and obedient, he did exactly as he was told.

In the evening the old woman sent him into the garden to choose one of the drums which stood there. She warned him: "If you come to a drum which says 'Ding-ding' on being touched – take it. But be very careful not to cake one which sounds 'Dong-dong,' "He obeyed her direction in every detail. When he showed her the drum, she looked pleased and told him, to his great delight, that he had only to beat it if at any time he were hungry. That would bring him food in plenty. He thanked the old woman very heartily and went home.

As soon as he reached his own hut, he gathered his household together, and then beat the drum. Immediately, food of every description appeared before them, and they all ate as much as they wished.

The following day Kwaku Tsin gathered all the people of the village together in the Assembly Place, and then beat the drum once more. In this way every family got sufficient food for their wants, and all thanked Kwaku very much for thus providing for them.

Kwaku's father, however, was not at all pleased to see his son thus to feed the whole village. Anansi thought he, too, ought to have a drum. Then the people would be grateful to him instead of to Kwaku Tsin. Accordingly, he asked the young man where the wonderful drum had come from. His son was most unwilling to tell him, but Anansi gave him no peace until he had heard the whole story. He then wasted no time, but set off at once toward the entrance hole. He had taken the precaution to carry with him an old nut which he pretended to crack. Then throwing it into the hole, he jumped in after it and hurried along to the silent village. Arrived at the first house, he shouted, "Is there one in this town?"

The old woman answered as before, and Anansi entered her house.

He did not trouble to be polite to her, but addressed her most rudely, saying, "Hurry up, old woman, and get me something to eat." The woman quietly directed him to go into the garden and choose the yam which should say, "Do not dig me out." Anansi laughed in her face and said, "You surely take me for a fool. If the yam does not want me to dig it out I will certainly not do so. I will take the one which wants to be gathered." This he did.

When he brought it to the old woman she told him, as she told his son, to throw away the inside and boiled the rind. Again he refused to obey. "Who ever heard of such silly thing as throwing away the yam? I will do nothing of sort. I will throw away the peel and boil the inside. He did so, and the yam turned into stones. He was then obliged to do as she first suggested, and boil the rind. The latter while boiling turned into yam. Anansi turned angrily to the old woman and said, "You are a witch." She took no notice of his remark, but went on setting the table. She placed his dinner on a small table, lower than her own saying, "You must not look at me while I eat." He rudely replied, "Indeed, I will look at you if I choose. And I will have my dinner

at your table, not at that small one." Again she said nothing – but she left her dinner untouched. Anansi ate his meal, then took hers and ate it also.

When he had finished she said, "Now go into the garden and choose a drum. Do not take one which sounds 'Dong-dong'; only take one which says 'Ding-ding.' Anansi retorted, "Do not think I will take your advice, you witch? No I will choose the drum says 'Dong-dong.' You are just trying to play trick on me."

He did as he wished. Having secured the drum he marched off without so much as a "Thank you" to the old woman.

No sooner had he reached home, than he longed to show off his new power to the villagers. He called all to the Assembly Place, telling them to bring dishes and trays, as he was going to provide them with food. The people in great delight buried to the spot. Anansi, proudly taking his position in the midst of them to beat his drum. To his horror and dismay, instead of the multitude of food-stuffs which Kwaku had summoned, Anansi saw, rushing toward him, beasts and serpents of all kinds. Such creatures had never been seen on the earth before.

The people fled in every direction – all except Anansi, who too terrified to move. He speedily received fitting punishment for his disobedience. Fortunately, Kwaku, with his mother and sisters, had been at the outer edge of the crowd, so easily escaped into shelter. The animals presently scattered in every direction, and ever since they have roamed wild in the great forests.

HONOURABLE MINŪ

IT happened one day that a poor Akim-man had to travel from his own little village to Accra – one of the big towns on the coast. This man could only speak the language of his own village – As he approached Accra he met a great herd of cows. He was surprised at the number of them, and wondered to whom they could belong. Seeing a man with them he asked him. "To whom do these cows belong?" The man did not know the language of the Akim-man, so he replied, "Minu" (I do not understand). The Traveller, however, thought that Minu was the name of the owner of the cows and exclaimed. "Mr. Minu must be very rich."

He then entered the town. Very soon he saw a fine large building, and wondered to whom it might belong. The man he asked could not understand his question so he also answered, "Minu." "Dear me! What a rich fellow Mr. Minu must be!" cried the Akim-man.

Coming to a still finer building with beautiful gardens round it, he again asked the owner's name. Again came the answer,

"Minu." "How wealthy Mr. Minu is," said our wondering traveller.

Next he came to the beach. There he saw a magnificent steamer being loaded in the harbour. He was surprised at the great cargo which was being put on board and inquired of a bystander, "To whom does this fine vessel belong?" "Minu", replied the man. "To the Honourable Minu also! He is the richest man I ever heard of!" cried the Akim-man.

Having finished his business, the Akim-man set out for home. As he passed down one of the streets of the town he met carrying a coffin, and followed by a long procession, all dressed in black. He asked the name of the dead person, and received the usual reply, "Minu." "Poor Mr. Minu!" cried the Akim-man. "So he has had to leave all his wealth and beautiful houses and die just as a poor person would do! Well, well – in future I will be content with my tiny house and little money." And the Akim-man went home quite pleased to his own hut.

WHY THE MOON AND THE STARS RECEIVE THEIR LIGHT FROM THE SUN

ONCE upon a time there was great scarcity of food in the land. Father Anansi and his son, Kwaku Tsin, being very hungry, set out one morning to hunt in the forest. In a short time Kwaku Tsin was fortunate enough to kill a fine antelope – which he carried to his father at their resting-place. Anansi was very glad to see such a supply of food, and requested his son to remain there on guard, while he went for a large basket in which to carry it home. An hour or so passed without his return, and Kwaku Tsin became anxious. Fearing lest his father had lost his way, he called out loudly, "Father, father!" to guide him to the spot. To his joy he heard a voice reply, "Yes, my son," and immediately he shouted again, thinking it was Anansi. Instead of the latter, however, a terrible dragon appeared. This monster breathed fire from his great nostrils, and was altogether a dreadful sight to behold. Kwaku Tsin was terrified at his approach and speedily hid himself in a cave nearby.

The dragon arrived at the resting-place, and was much annoyed to find only the antelope's body. He vented his anger in blows upon the latter and went away. Soon after, Father Anansi made his appearance. He was greatly interested in his son's tale, and wished to see the dragon for himself. He soon had his desire, for the monster, smelling human flesh, hastily returned to the spot and seized them both. They were carried off by him to his castle, where they found many other unfortunate creatures also awaiting their fate. All were left in charge of the dragon's servant – a fine, white cock – which always crowed to summon his master, if anything unusual happened in the latter's absence. The dragon then went off in search of more prey.

Kwaku Tsin now summoned all his fellow-prisoners together, to arrange a way of escape. All feared to run away-because of the wonderful powers of the monster. His eyesight was so keen that he could detect a fly moving miles away. Not only that, but he could move over the ground so swiftly that none could outdistance him. Kwaku Tsin, however, being exceedingly clever, soon thought of a plan.

Knowing that the white cock would not crow as long as he had grains of rice to pick up, Kwaku scattered on the ground the contents of forty bags of grain – which were stored in the great hall. While the cock was thus busily engaged, Kwaku Tsin ordered the spinners to spin fine hempen ropes, to make a strong ladder. One end of this be intended to throw up to heaven, trusting that the gods would catch it and hold it fast, while he and his fellow-prisoners mounted.

While the ladder was being made, the men killed and ate all the cattle they needed – reserving all the bones for Kwaku Tsin at his express desire. When all was ready the young man gathered the bones into a great sack. He also procured the dragon's fiddle and placed it by his side.

Everything was now ready. Kwaku Tsin threw one end of the ladder up to the sky. It was caught and held. The dragon's victims began to mount, one after the other, Kwaku remaining at the bottom.

By this time, however, the monster's powerful eye sight showed him that something unusual was happening at his abode. He hastened his return. On seeing his approach, Kwaku Tsin also mounted the ladder – with the bag of bones on his back, and the fiddle under his arm. The dragon began to climb after him. Each time the monster came too near the young man threw him a bone, with which, being very hungry, he was obliged to descend to the ground to eat.

Kwaku Tsin repeated this performance till all the bones were gone, by which time the people were safely up in heavens. Then he mounted himself rapidly as possible, stopping every now and then to play a tune on the wonderful fiddle. Each time he did this, the dragon had to return to earth, to dance – as he could not resist the magic music. When Kwaku was quite close to the top, the dragon had very nearly reached him again. The brave youth bent down and cut the ladder away below his own feet. The dragon was dashed to the ground – but Kwaku was pulled up into safety by the gods.

The latter were so pleased with his wisdom and bravery in giving freedom to his fellow-men, that they made him the sun – the source of all light and heat to the world. His father, Anansi, became the moon, and his friends the stars. Thereafter, it was Kwaku Tsin's privilege to supply all these with light, each being dull and powerless without him.

OBENG AND THE
THIEVING ANTELOPE

THERE once lived upon the earth a poor man called Obeng, whose wife was named Awusi. This unfortunate couple had suffered one troubled after another. No matter what they took in hand misfortune seemed to lie in wait for them. Nothing they did met with success. They became so poor that at last they could scarcely obtain a cloth with which to cover themselves.

Finally, Obeng thought of a plan which many of his neighbours had tried and found successful. He went to a wealthy farmer who lived near, and offered to hew down several of his palm-trees. He would then collect their sap to make palm wine. When this should be ready for the market, his wife would carry it there and sell it. The proceeds would then be divided equally between the farmer, Obeng, and Awusi.

This proposal having been laid before the farmer, he proved quite willing to agree to it. Not only so, but he granted Obeng a supply of earthen pots in which to collect the sap, as the miserable man was far too poor to buy any.

In great delight Obeng and his wife set to work. They cut down the trees and prepared them –setting the pots underneath to catch the sap. Before cockcrow on markets day, Obeng set off, with a lighted torch, to collect the wine and prepare it for his wife to take into the town. She was almost ready to follow.

To his great distress, on arriving at the first tree, instead of finding his earthen pot filled with the sweet sap, he saw it lying in pieces on the ground –the wine all gone. He went on to the second and third trees –but there, and at all the others, too, the same thing happened.

His wife, in high spirits and ready for market, joined him at this moment. She saw at once by his face that some misfortune had again befallen them. Sorrowfully, they examined the mischief, and agreed that some wicked person had stolen the wine and then broken the pots to hide the theft. Awusi returned home in despair, but Obeng set to work once more. He fetched a second supply of pots and placed them all ready to catch the sap.

On his return next morning, he found that the same behavior had been repeated. All his wine was again stolen and his pots in fragments. He had no resource but to go to the farmer and tell him of these fresh misfortunes. The farmer proved to be very kind and generous and gave others that Obeng might have as many pots as he should require.

Once more the poor fellow returned to the palm-trees, and set his pots ready. This third attempt, however, met with no better result than the two previous. Obeng went home in despair. His wife was of the opinion that they should give up trying to overcome their evil fortunes. It was quite evident that they could never attain success. The husband, however, determined that, at least, he would find and punish the culprit, if that were possible.

Accordingly, he bravely set his pots in order for the last time. When night came, he remained on guard among the trees. Midnight passed and nothing happened, but toward two o'clock in the morning a dark form glided past him to the nearest palm-tree. A moment after he heard the sound of a breaking pot. He stole up to the form. On approaching it he found that the thief was a bush-antelope, carrying on its head a large jar, into which it was pouring the wine from Obeng's pots. As it emptied them it threw them carelessly on the ground, breaking them in pieces.

Obeng ventured a little nearer, intending to seize the culprit. The latter, however, was too quick for him and escaped, dropping his great pot on the ground as he ran. The antelope was very fleet, but Obeng had fully determined to catch him – so followed. The chase continued over many miles until mid-day arrived, at which time they had reached the bottom of a high hill. The antelope immediately began to climb, and Obeng – though almost tired out – still followed. Finally, the summit of the hill was reached, and there Obeng found himself in the midst of a great gathering of quadrupeds. The antelope, panting, threw himself on the ground before King Leopard. His Majesty commanded that Obeng should be brought before him to be punished for this intrusion into such a serious meeting.

Obeng begged for a hearing before they condemned him. He wished to explain fully his presence there. King Leopard, after consulting with some of the other animals, agreed to listen to his tale. Thereupon Obeng began the story of his unfortunate life. He told how one trial after another had failed, and how, finally, he had thought of the palm wine. He described his feelings on discovering the first theft –after all his labour. He related his second, third, and fourth attempts, with the result of each. He then went on to tell of the chase after the thief, and thus explained his presence at their conference.

The quadrupeds listened very attentively to the recital of Obeng's troubles. At the conclusion they unanimously agreed that the antelope was the culprit and the man blameless. The former was accordingly sentenced to punishment, while the latter received an apology in the name of the entire conference. King Leopard, it appeared, had each morning given Antelope a large sum of money wherewith to purchase palm wine for the whole assembly. The antelope had stolen the wine and kept the money.

To make up to Obeng for his losses, King Leopard offered him, as a gift, the power of understanding the conversation of all animals. This, said he, would speedily make Obeng a rich man. But he attached one condition to the gift. Obeng must never – on pain of instant death – tell anyone about his wonderful power.

The poor man, much delighted, set off for home. When it was reached, he lost no time in setting to work at his palm-trees again. From that day his troubles seemed over. His wine was never interfered with and he and Awusi became more and more prosperous and happy.

One morning, while he was bathing in a pool quite close to his house, he heard a hen and her chickens talking together in his garden. He listened, and distinctly heard a chicken tell Mother

Hen about three jars of gold buried in Obeng's garden. The hen bade the chicken be careful, lest her master should see her scraping near the gold, and so discover it.

Obeng pretended to take no notice of what they were saying, and went away. Presently, when Mother Hen and her brood had gone, he came back and commenced digging in that part of the garden. To his great joy, he soon found three large jars of gold. They contained enough money to keep him in comfort all his life. He was careful, however, not to mention his treasure to anyone but his wife. He bid it safely inside his house.

Soon he and Awusi had become one of the richest couples in the neighbourhood, and owned quite a large amount of property. Obeng thought he could afford now to keep a second wife, so he married again. Unfortunately, the new wife did not at all resemble Awusi. The latter had always been a good, kind, honest woman. The new wife was of a very jealous and selfish disposition. In addition to this she was lame, and continually imagined that people were making fun of her defect. She took the idea into her head that Obeng and Awusi – when together – were in the habit of laughing at her. Nothing was further from their thought, but she refused to believe so. Whenever she saw them together she would stand and listen outside the door to hear what they were saying. Of course, she never succeeded in hearing anything about herself.

At last, one evening, Obeng and Awusi had gone to bed. The latter was fast asleep when Obeng heard a conversation which amused him very much. A couple of mice in one corner of the room were arranging to go to the larder to get some food, as soon as their master – who was watching them – was asleep. Obeng, thinking this was a good joke, laughed outright. His lame wife heard him, and rushed into the room. She thereupon accused him of making fun of her again to Awusi. The astonished husband, of course, denied this, but to no purpose. The jealous woman insisted that, if he were laughing at an innocent joke, he would at once tell it to her. This Obeng could not do, without breaking his promise to King Leopard. His refusal fully confirmed the lame woman's suspicions and she did not rest till she had laid the whole matter before the chief. He being an intimate friend of Obeng, tried to persuade him to reveal the joke and set the matter at rest. Obeng naturally was most unwilling to do anything of the sort. The persistent woman gave the chief no peace till he summoned her husband to answer her charge before the assembly.

Finding no way of escape from the difficulty, Obeng prepared for death. He first called all his friends and relatives to a great feast, and bade them farewell. Then he put his affairs in order – bequeathed all his gold to the faithful Awusi, and his property to his son and servants. When he had finished, he went to the Assembly Place where the people of the neighbourhood were gathered together.

He first took leave of the chief, and then commenced his tale. He related the story of his many misfortunes – of his adventure with the antelope, and of his promise to King Leopard. Finally, he explained the cause of his laughter which had annoyed his wife. In so speaking he fell dead, as the Leopard had warned him.

He was buried amid great mourning, for everyone had liked and respected him. The jealous woman who had caused her husband's death was seized and burnt as a witch. Her ashes were then scattered to the four winds of heaven, and it owes to this unfortunate fact that jealousy and selfishness are so widespread through the world, where before they scarcely existed.

HOW THE TORTOISE
GOT ITS SHELL

A FEW hundred years ago, the Chief Mauri (God) determined to have a splendid yam festival. He therefore sent his messengers to invite all his chiefs and people to the gathering, which was to take place on Fida (Friday).

On the morning of that day he sent some of his servants to the neighbouring towns and villages to buy goats, sheep, and cows for the great feast. Mr. Klo (the tortoise), who was a tall and handsome fellow, was sent to buy palm wine. He was directed to the palm-fields of Koklovi (the chicken).

At that time Klo was a very powerful traveller and speedily reached his destination, although it was many miles distant from Mauri's palace.

When he arrived Koklovi was taking his breakfast. When they had exchanged polite salutations Koklovi asked the reason of Klo's visit. He replied, "I was sent by His Majesty Mauri, the ruler of the world, to buy him palm wine." "Whether he's ruler of the world or not," answered Koklovi, "no one can buy my wine with money. If you want it you must fight for it. If you win you can have it all and the palm-trees too."

This answer delighted Klo as he was a very strong fighter. Koklovi was the same, so that the fighting continued for several hours before Klo was able to overcome Koklovi. He was at last successful, however, and securely bound Koklovi before he left him.

Then, taking his great pot, he filled it with wine. Finding that there was more than the pot would hold, Klo foolishly drank all the rest. He then piled the palm-trees on his back and set out for the palace with the pot of wine. The amount which he had drunk, however, made him feel so sleepy and tired that he could not walk fast with his load. Added to this, a terrible rain began to fall, which made the ground very slippery and still more difficult to travel over.

By the time Klo successes in reaching his master's palace the gates were shut and locked. Mauri, finding it so late, had concluded that everyone was inside.

There were many people packed into the great hall, and all were singing and dancing. The noise of the concert was so great that no one heard Klo's knocking at the gate, and there he had to stay with his great load and palm trees.

The rain continued for nearly two months and was so terrible that the people all remained in the palace till it had finished. By that time Klo had died, under the weight of his load –which he had been unable to get off his back. There he lay, before the gate, with the pile of palm-trees on top of him.

When the rain ceased and the gates were opened the people were amazed to see this great mound in from of the gate, where before there had been nothing. They fetched spades and began to shovel it away.

When they came to the bottom of the pile there lay Klo. His earthenware pot and the dust had caked together and formed quite a hard cover on his back.

He was taken into the palace – and by the use of many wonderful medicines he was restored to life. But since that date he has never been able to stand upright. He has been a creeping creature, with a great shell on his back.

THE HUNTER
AND THE TORTOISE

A VILLAGE hunter had one day gone farther afield than usual. Coming to a part of the forest with which he was unacquainted, he was astonished to hear a voice singing. He listened; this was the song.

> "It is man who forces himself on things,
>
> Not thing which force themselves on him."

The singing was accompanied by sweet music – which entirely charmed the hunter's heart.

When the little song was finished, the hunter peeped through the branches to see who the singer could be. Imagine his amazement when he found it was none other than a tortoise, with a tiny harp slung in front of her. Never had he seen such a marvelous thing.

Time after time he returned to the same place in order to listen to this wonderful creature. At last he persuaded her to let him carry her back to his hut, that he might enjoy her singing daily comfort. This she permitted, only on the understanding that she sang to him alone.

The hunter did not rest long content with this arrangement, however. Soon he began to wish that he could show off this wonderful tortoise to all the world, and thereby thought he would gain great honour. He told the secret, first to one, then to another, unto finally it reached the ears of the chief himself. The hunter was commanded to come and tell his tale before the Assembly. When, however, he described the tortoise that sang and played on the harp, the people shouted in scorn. They refused to believe him.

At last he said, "If I do not speak truth, I give you leave to kill me. Tomorrow I will bring the tortoise to this place and you may all hear her. If she cannot do as I say, I am willing to die." "good," replied the people, "and if the tortoise can do as you say, we give you leave to punish us in any way you choose."

The matter being then settled, the hunter returned home, well pleased with the prospect. As soon as the morrow dawned, he carried tortoise and harp down to the Assembly Place – where a table had been placed ready for her. Every one gathered round to listen. But no song came. The people were very patient, and quite willing to give both tortoise and hunter a chance. Hours went by, and, to the hunter dismay and shame, the tortoise remained mute.

He tried every means in his power to coax her to sing, but in vain. The people at first whispered, then spoke outright, in scorn of the boaster and his claims.

Night came on and brought with it the hunter's doom. As the last ray of the setting sun faded, he was beheaded. The instant this had happened the tortoise spoke. The people looked at one another in troubled wonder: "Our brother spoke truth, then, and we have killed him." The tortoise, however, went on to explain. "He brought his punishment on himself. I led a happy life in the forest, singing my little song. He was not content to come and listen to me. He had to tell my secret (which did not at all concern him) to all the world. Had he not tried to make a show of me this would never have happened.

"It is man who forces himself on things,

Not thing which force themselves on him."

THE TAIL OF
THE PRINCESS ELEPHANT

THERE once lived a woman who had three sons. These sons were very much attached to their mother and always tried to please her. She at last grew very old and feeble. The three sons began to think what they could do to give her great pleasure. The eldest promised that when she was dead he would cut a fine sepulcher in stone for her. The second said he would make a beautiful coffin. The youngest said, "I will go and get the tail of the princes elephant and put it in the coffin with her." This promise was by far the hardest one to keep.

Soon after this their mother died. The youngest son immediately set out on his search, not knowing in the least where he would be likely to find the tail. He travelled for three weeks, and at the end of that time he came to a little village. There he met an old woman, who seemed very much surprised to see him. She said no human creature had even been there before. The boy told the tale of his search for the princess elephant. The old woman replied that this village was the home of all the elephants, and the princess slept there every night. But she warned him that if the animals saw him they would kill him. The young man begged her to hide him – which she did, in a great pile of wood.

She also told that when the elephants were all asleep he must get up and go to the eastern corner. There he would find the princess. He must walk boldly over, cut off the tail and return in the same manner. If he were to walk stealthily, the elephants would waken and seize him.

The animals returned as it was growing dark. They said at once that they smelt a human being. The old woman assured them that they were mistaken. Their supper was ready, so they ate it and went to bed.

In the middle of the night the young man got up and walked boldly across to where the princess slept. He cut off the tail and returned as he had come. He then started for home, carrying the tail very carefully.

When daylight came the elephants awoke. One said he had dreamed that the princess's tail was stolen. The others beat him for thinking such a thing. A second said he also had the dream, and he also was beaten. The wisest of the elephants then suggested that they might do well to go and see if the dream were true. This they did. They found the princess fast asleep and quite ignorant of the loss of her tail. They wakened her and all started off in chase of the young man.

They travelled so quickly that in a few hours they came in sight of him. He was afraid when he saw them coming and cried out to his favourite idol (which he always carried in his hair), "O my juju Depor! What shall I do?" The juju advised him to throw the branch of a tree over his shoulder. This he did and it immediately grew up into a huge tree, which blocked the path of the elephants. They stopped and began to eat up the tree – which took them some little time.

Then they continued their way again. Again the young man cried, "O my juju Depor! What shall I do?" "Throw that corn-cob behind you," answered the juju. The lad did so, and the corn-cob immediately grew into a large field of maize.

The elephants ate their way through the maize. But when they arrived at the other side they found that the boy had reached home. So they had to give up the chase and return to their village. The princess, however, refused to do so, saying, "I will return when I have punished this impudent fellow."

She thereupon changed herself into a very beautiful maiden, and taking a calabash cymbal in her hand approached the village. All the people came out to admire this lovely girl.

She had it proclaimed through the village that whoever succeeded in shooting an arrow at the cymbal should have her for a bride. The young men all tried and failed. An old man standing by said, "If only Kwasi – the cutter of the princess elephant's tail – were here, he could hit the cymbal." "Then Kwasi is the man I will marry," replied the maiden, "whether he hit the cymbal or not."

Kwasi was quickly fetched from the field where he was ploughing, and told of his good luck. He, however, was not at all delighted to hear of it, as he suspected the maiden of some trick.

However, he came and shot an arrow which struck the centre of the cymbal. The damsel and he were accordingly married. She was all time preparing to punish him.

The night following their marriage she turned into an elephant, while Kwasi was asleep. She then prepared to kill him, but Kwasi awoke in time. He called, "O my juju Depor! Save me!" The juju turned him into a grass mat lying on the bed and the princess could not find him. She was most annoyed and next morning asked him where he had been all night. "While you were an elephant I was the mat you lay on," replied Kwasi. The damsel took all the mats from the bed and burned them.

Next night the princess again became an elephant and prepared to kill her husband. This time the juju changed him into a needle and his wife could not find him. She again asked him in the morning where he had been. Hearing that the juju had helped him again she determined to get hold of the idol and destroy it.

Next day Kwasi was going again to his farm to plough field. He told his wife to bring him some food to the resting-place. This time she had fairly made up her mind that he should not escape. When he had his food she said, "Now lay your head in my lap and sleep." Kwasi quite forgot that his juju was hidden in his hair and did as she bid. As soon as he was asleep she took the juju out of his hair and threw it into a great fire which she had prepared. Kwasi awoke to find her an elephant once more. In great feat he cried out, "O my juju Depor! What am I to do?" All the answer he got, however, came from the flames. "I am burning, I am burning, I am burning." Kwasi called again for help and the juju replied, "Lift up your arms as if you were flying." He did so and turned into a hawk.

That is the reason why hawks are so often seen flying in the smoke of fires. They are looking for their lost juju.

KOFI AND THE GODS

KOFI was the eldest son of a farmer who had two wives. Kofi's mother had no other children.

When the boy was three years old his mother died. Kofi was given to his stepmother to mind. After this she had many children. Kofi, of course, was the eldest of all.

When he was about ten years old his father also died. Kofi had no relative but his stepmother, for whom he had to work.

As he grew older, she saw how much more clever and handsome he was than her own children, and grew very jealous of him. He was such a good hunter that day after day he came home laden with meat and fish.

Every day she treated him in the same way. She cooked the meat, then portioned it out. She gave to each a large helping, but when it came to Kofi's turn she would say, "oh my son Kofi, there is none left for you! You must go to the field and get some ripe paw-paw." Kofi never complained. Never once did he taste any of the meat he had hunted. At every meal the others were served, but there was never enough for him.

One evening, when the usual thing had happened, Kofi was preparing to go to the field to fetch some paw-paw for his supper. All at once , one of the gods appeared in the village, carrying a great bag over his shoulder. He summoned all the villagers together with these words: "Oh, my villagers, I come with a bag of death for you!"

Thereupon he began to distribute the contents of his bag among them. When he came to Kofi he said: "Oh, my son Kofi, there was never sufficient meat for you, neither is there any death."

As he said these words everyone in the village died except Kofi. He was left to reign there in peace, which he did very happily.

THE LION AND THE WOLF

A CERTAIN old lady had a very fine flock of sheep. She had fed and cared for them so well that they became famous for their fatness. In time a wicked wolf heard of them and determined to eat them.

Night after night he stole up to the old dame's cottage and killed a sheep. The poor woman tried her best to save her animals from harm – but failed.

At last there was only one sheep left of all the flock. Their owner was very sad. She feared that it, too, would be taken away from her, in spite of all she could do. While she was grieving over the thought of this a lion came to her village.

Seeing her sad face, he asked the reason of it. She soon told him all about it. He thereupon offered to do his best to punish the wicked wolf. He himself went to the place where the sheep was generally kept –while the latter was removed to another place.

In the meantime the wolf was on his way to the cottage. As he came he met a fox. The fox was somewhat afraid of him and prepared to run away. The wolf, however, told him where he was going, and invited him to go too. The fox agreed and the two set off together. They arrived at the cottage and went straight to the place where the sheep generally slept. The wolf at once rushed upon the animal, while fox waited a little behind. Just as fox was deciding to enter and help wolf there came a bright flash of lighting. By the light of it the fox could see that the wolf was attacking – not a sheep – but a lion. He hastily ran away, shouting as he went: "Look at his face! Look at his face!"

During the flash wolf did look at the pretended sheep. To his dismay he found he had made a great mistake. At once he began to make humble apologies – but all in vain. Lion refused to listen to any of his explanations, and speedily put him to death.

MAKU MAWU AND MAKU FIĀ

ONCE upon a time there were two men who were such great friends that they were almost together. If one was seen the other was sure to be near. They had given one another special names, which were to be used only by themselves. One name, Maki Mawu, meant, 'I will die God's death,' and the other, Maku Fia, 'I will die the King's death.'

By and by, however, the other villagers heard these names and gradually everyone got into the habit of calling the two friends by the nicknames in preference to the real ones. Finally, the King of the country heard of them and wished to see the men who had chosen such strange titles. He sent for them to Court, and they came together. He was much pleased with the one who had chosen the name of 'Maku Fia,' but he was annoyed at the other man's choice and sought a chance of punishing him.

When he had talked to them a little while, he invited both to a great feast which he was to give in three day's time. As they went away he gave fine large yam to Maku Mawu and only a small round stone to his own favourite. The latter felt somewhat aggrieved at getting only a stone, while his friend got such a fine yam. Very soon he said, "Oh, dear! I do not think it is any use carrying this stone home. How I wish it were a yam! Then I could cook it for dinner." Maku Mawu – being very generous – immediately replied, "Then change with me, for I am quite tired of carrying my great yam." They exchanged, and each went off to his own home. Maku Fia cut up his yam and cooked it. Maku Mawu broke his stone in half and found inside some beautiful ornaments which the King had hidden there. He thought that he would play a trick on the King, so told nobody what had been in the stone.

On the third day they dressed to go to the King's feast. Maku Mawu put on all the beautiful ornaments out of the stone. Maku Fia dressed himself just as usual.

When they reached the palace the King was amazed to see the wrong man wearing his ornaments, and determined to punish him more effectually next time. He asked Maku Fia what he had done with the stone, and the man told him he had exchanged it for his friend's yam.

At first the King could not think of any way to punish Maku Mawu, as, of course, the latter had not done anything wrong. He soon had an idea, however. He pretended to be very pleased with the poor man and presented him with a beautiful ring from his own finger. He then made him promise to come back in seven days and show the ring to the King again, to let the latter see that it was not lost. If by any chance he could not produce the ring – he would lose his head. This the King did, meaning to get hold of the ring in some way and so get the young man killed.

Maku Mawu saw that the King's design was, so determined to hide the ring. He made a small hole in the wall of his room, put the ring in it, and carefully plastered over the place again. No one could see that the wall had been touched.

After two days the King sent for the wife of Maku Mawu and asked to find the ring. He promised her a large sum of money for it – not telling her, of course, what would happen to her husband if the ring were lost. The woman went home and searched diligently but found nothing. Next day she tried again – with no better success. Then she asked her husband what he had done with it. He innocently told her it was in the wall. Next day, when he was absent, she searched so carefully that at last she found it.

Delighted, she ran off to the King's palace and gave the ring to him. She got the promised money and returned home, never dreaming that she had really sold her husband's life.

On the sixth day the King sent a message to Maku Mawu, telling him to prepare for the next day. The poor man bethought himself of the ring and went to look if it were still safe. To his despair the hole was empty. He asked his wife and his neighbours. All denied having seen it. He made up his mind that he must die.

In the meantime the King had laid the ring in one of the dishes in his palace and promptly forgot about it. When the seventh morning had arrived he sent messengers far and wide, to summon the people to come and see a man punished for disobeying the King's order. Then he commanded his servants to set the palace in order, and to take the dishes out of his room and wash them.

The careless servants – never looking to see if the dishes were empty or not –took them all to a pool nearby. Among them was the dish containing the ring. Of course, when the dish was being washed, out fell the ring into the water – without being noticed by the servants.

The palace being all in readiness, the King went to fetch the ring. It was nowhere to be found and he was obliged to go to the Assembly without it.

When everyone was ready the poor man, Maku Mawu, was called to come forward to show the ring. He walked boldly up to the king and knelt down before him, saying, "The ring is lost and I am prepared to die. Only grant me a few hours to put my house in order." At first the king was unwilling to grant even that small favour, but finally he said, "Very well, you may have four hours. Then you must return here and beheaded before the people." The innocent man returned to his home and put everything in order. Then, feeling hungry, he thought, "I may as well have some food before I die. I will go and catch a fish in the pool."

He accordingly took his fish-net and bait, and started off to the very pool where the King's dishes had been washed. Very soon he caught a fine large fish. Cutting it open, to clean it, his delight may be imagined at finding the lost ring inside it.

At once he ran off to the palace crying: "I have found the ring! I have found the ring!" When the people heard him, they all shouted in joy: "He named himself rightly 'Maku Mawu,' for see – the death God has chosen for him, that only will he die." So the King had no excuse to harm him, and he went free.

THE ROBBER
AND THE OLD MAN

IN a big town lived a very rich gentleman. The fame of his wealth soon spread. A clever thief heard of it and determined to have some for himself.

He managed to hide himself in a dark corner of the gentleman's room – while the latter was counting his bags of money. As soon as the old gentleman left the room to fetch something, the thief caught up two of the bags and escaped.

The owner was astonished, on his return a few minutes later, to find two bags short. He could find no trace of the thief.

Next morning, however, he chanced to meet the robber just outside the house. The dishonest man looked so confused that the rich man at once suspected he was the thief. He could not, however, prove it, so took the case before the judge.

The thief was much alarmed when he heard this. He sought a man in the village and asked his advice. The wise man undertook to help him – if he would promise to pay him half the money when he got off. This robber at once said he would do.

The old man then advised him to go home and dress in rags. He must ruffle his hair and beard and behave as if he were mad. If anyone asked a question he must answer "Moo."

The thief did so. To every question asked by the judge he said, "Moo, moo." The judge at last grew angry and dismissed the court. The thief went home in great glee.

Next day, the wise man came to him for his half of the stolen money. But he could get no answer but "Moo" from the thief, and at last, in despair, he had to go home without a penny. The ungrateful robber kept everything for himself. The wise man regretted very much that he had to go home without a penny. The wise man regretted very much that he had saved the thief from his just punishment – but it was now too late.

THE LEOPARD AND THE RAM

A RAM once decided to make a clearing in the woods and build himself a house. A leopard who lived near also made up his mind to do the very same thing.

Unknown to each other they both chose the same site. Ram came one day and worked at the clearing. Leopard arrived after Ram had gone and was much surprised to find some of his work already done. However, he continued what Ram had begun. Each was daily surprised at the progress made in his absence, but concluded that the spirits had been helping him. He gave them thanks and continued with his task.

Thus the matter went on – the two working alternately at the building and never seeing one another. At last the house was finished to the satisfaction of both.

The two prepared to take up their abode in the new home. To their great astonishment they met. Each told his tale, and after some friendly discussion, they decided to live together.

Both Leopard and Ram had sons. These two young animals played together while their parents hunted. The leopard was very much surprised to find that every evening his friend Ram brought home just as much meat or venison from the hunt as he himself did. He did not dare, however, to ask the other how he obtained it.

One day, before setting out to hunt, Leopard requested his son to find out, if possible, from young Ram, how his father managed to kill the animals. Accordingly while they were at play, little Leopard inquired how Father Ram, having neither claws nor sharp teeth, succeeded in catching and killing the beasts. Ram refused to tell unless young Leopard would promise to show his father's way also. The latter agreed. Accordingly they took large pieces of plantain stem and set out into the woods.

Young Leopard then took one piece and placed it in position. Then, going first to the right, then to the left – bowing and standing on his hind legs and peeping at the stem just as his father did – he took aim, sprang toward the stem and tore it.

Young Ram then took the other piece and placed it in position. Wasting no time he went backward a little way, took aim, then ran swiftly forward – pushing his head against the stem and tearing it to pieces. When they had finished they swept the place clean and went home.

In the evening the leopard obtained all the information about the hunt from his son. The latter warned him that he must always be careful when he saw the ram go backward. He kept this in mind, and from that day watched the ram very closely.

Some time afterward it rained, making the floor of the house very slippery. The leopard called the ram, as usual, to dine with him. As he was coming, the ram slipped backward on the next floor. The leopard, seeing this, thought the other was about to kill him. Calling to his son to follow, he sprang with all his might over the wall of the house and fled to the woods. The ram called him back, but he did not listen. From that time leopards have made their abode in the woods while rams have remained at home.

WHY THE LEOPARD
CAN ONLY CATCH PREY
ON ITS LEFT SIDE

AT one time leopards did not know how to catch animals for food. Knowing that the cat was very skilful in this way, Leopard one day went to Cat and asked very politely if she would teach him the art. Cat readily consented.

The first thing Leopard had to learn was to hide himself among the bushes by the roadside, so that he would not be seen by any animal passing by. Next he must learn how to move noiselessly through the woods. He must never allow the animal he chased to know that he was following it. The third great principle was how to use his left paws and side in springing upon his prey.

Having taught him these three things, Cat requested him to go and practice them well. When he had learnt them thoroughly he could return to her and she would give him more lessons in hunting.

Leopard obeyed. At first he was very successful and obtained all the food he wanted. One day, however, he was unable to catch anything at all. Being very hungry, he bethought himself what he could have for dinner. Suddenly he remembered that cat had quite a large family. He went straight to her home and found her absent.

Never thinking of her kindness to him – Leopard only remembered that he was hungry – he ate all her kittens. Puss, on discovering this dreadful fact, was so angry that she refused to have anything more to do with the great creature.

Consequently the leopard has never been able to learn how to catch animals that pass him on the right side.

KWAKU BAH-BONI, THE BAD BOY

ONCE upon a time in a certain village lived a man and his wife who were childless. One day, however, when the husband was away hunting, the woman had a baby son. She was greatly troubled at her husband's absence, because she was unable to let him know of the child's arrival. In that country it is the custom for the father to give the baby its name when it is a week old. As the time approached for the naming, the woman wondered to herself what name she could give the child if her husband did not return in time. To her amazement, the child himself answered, "My name is Kwaku Bah-boni." As he was only a week old she was astonished to hear him talk. The next day she got a greater surprise. She had been grumbling because her husband was not there to go to the farm for her and fetch food. The baby announced, "I will go to the farm" – which he did.

When he was a few weeks old, she was one day very busy. She laid him down on the bed while she went on with her task. In a few minutes several boys came up to her in great anger. "Your son has beating us and ill-treating us in the street," said they. "My son!" she cried. "Why, my son is only a tiny baby. He is lying asleep on my bed." To convince them she went indoors to show them the baby. Imagine her surprise when he was nowhere to be seen! She had to apologize to the boys and beg them to forgive the child. Shortly after, he came in and put himself to bed.

He continued these mischievous tricks till his mother could no longer endure them. So she turned him out of the house and forbade him to return. He departed in great glee.

After walking a few miles, he came to a building where a goat, wolf, leopard, lion, and elephant lived very happily together. These animals were all sitting round their fire when he approached. After many polite speeches, he begged their permission to stay and be their servant, as he was motherless. The animals, after a little discussion, agreed to this, thinking that he would be able to help them in many ways. He was given a seat and some food, which he ate with great relish.

These five animals usually took it in turns to go out to their farm – a few miles away – every morning, to bring home food for the day. It being Goat's turn, he asked Kwaku to come with him to carry back the load.

The basket was accordingly handed to the little boy and he set off meekly after the goat. When they reached the farm, Kwaku set down the basket and ran off to play. He paid no heed at all to the goat's calls for assistance, but went on quietly playing. At last the goat was so annoyed that he came up to Kwaku and boxed his ears. To his great astonishment, the boy gave him such a blow that he fell to the ground. Kwaku then proceeded to beat him till the goat had promised to finish the work, carry home the load, and tell no one what had happened. Having promised this, the goat was allowed to go free. By this time the poor animal's face was bruised and swollen.

When the time came to go home the goat had to pack up the load and put it on his head. Then they set out.

As soon as they came in sight of their cottage, Kwaku took the basket from the goat and he himself carried it into the cottage.

The other animals all exclaimed in wonder when they saw the goat's face, and asked him how it had happened."I was unfortunate enough to get into a swarm of bees when I was working. They stung me," answered the poor goat.

Next day it was the wolf's turn to go to the farm. He also returned, much bruised and swollen. Goat (guessing what had happened) listened with a smile to the excuses made by Wolf to the others.

Goat and Wolf afterward talked the matter over and wondered much at the strength of the little boy.

Each day another animal took his turn at the farm, and each he returned in the same condition as his friends had done. At last all the animals had been, and all now came together to discuss how best they might get rid of Kwaku Bah-noni.

They made up their minds that, early the following morning, they would start off together and leave the boy in possession of the house. They prepared a big basket of food and set it ready.

Unfortunately for them, Kwaku had heard their discussion and decided that he also would go with them. He quietly got himself a large leaf, rolled it round him (for he was very tiny) and laid himself down in the basket of food.

At dawn the animals got up very quietly. Goat, being the youngest, was given the basket to carry. They started, feeling very thankful to get away from the tiresome boy – never dreaming that they were carrying him along with them.

When they had gone a fair distance Goat feeling very hot and tired, sat down to rest for a little while. As soon as the others had gone of sight, he opened the basket, meaning to have some food unknown to his friends. His greed was rewarded, however, by a terrible blow on the face. He then heard the words, "Shut the basket at once, and say nothing to the others." He obeyed and hurried after the others in fear of this terrible boy.

As soon as he reached them he called out, "Wolf, Wolf, it is your turn now to take the basket. I am very tired." Wolf took the load at once.

They had not gone far when Wolf began to think of all the nice things in the basket and he also said he was going to rest a little while in the shade. Having got rid of the others in this way, he hastily opened the basket. He was greeted by Kwaku in the same way as Goat had been, and speedily closed the basket and followed the others. In this way each animal got his turn of carrying the basket, and each was punished for his greed.

Finally, Elephant's turn came. When he rejoined the others and asked someone to relieve him of his load they cried out, "If you do not want to carry it any farther, throw it away." He did so, and they all took to their heels. They ran for several miles and only stopped when they came to a huge tree, in whose shade they sat down to rest, being quite breathless.

Kwaku , however, had got there before them. He had quietly stepped out of the basket, taken a short cut across country and arrived at the tree some time before them. He guessed that they would probably rest there – so he climbed up into the branches. There he remained, hidden among the leaves, while the animals sat on the ground below.

There they discussed Kwaku and all the trouble he had caused them. They blamed Goat for having been the one to persuade them to take the boy as a servant. Goat being the youngest of the company had the domestic work to do and he had welcomed the idea of help. Goat indignantly denied being the cause of all their troubles, saying:"If I am really to blame for the admission of Kwaku – let him appear before us." Kwaku promptly jumped down from the tree and stood in front of them. They were so alarmed at his appearance they scattered in all directions. The wolf ran to the woods – the leopard into the heart of forest, the elephant to Nigeria, the lion to desert, and the goat to the abode of human beings. That is the reason why they live now in these various places instead of all together as they did previously.

KING CHAMELEON
AND THE ANIMALS

IN the olden days all the animals of the world lived together in friendship. They had no one to rule over them and judge them. In consequence, many very wicked deeds were constantly being done, as no one needed to fear any punishment.

At last they all met together to discuss this bad state of affairs, and, as a result, they decided to choose a king. The great difficulty was how to choose him.

Lion was the first animal suggested. But all opposed him because, they said, he was too fierce. Wolf was next named – but the sheep and goats refused to have him because he was their foe. They knew they would have bad treatment if he were chosen.

As it was impossible to please everyone by choice, they decided in another way. Two miles away was a great stool, placed under a very ancient tree which they believed to be the abode of some of their gods. They would have a great race. The animal which reached and sat down first on the stool should be chosen king.

The day of the race arrived. All animals, great and small, prepared to take part in it. The signal being given, they started off. The hare – being a very fine runner – speedily outdistanced the others. He reached the stool quite five hundred yards ahead of the next animal. You may judge of his annoyance when, just as he was going to sit down, a voice came from the stool saying, "Take care, Mr. Hare, take care. I was here first." This was the chameleon. He, being able to change his colour to suit his surroundings, had seized Mr. Hare's tail just as the race began. Having made his colour march the hare's no one noticed him. He had held on very tightly, and when the hare turned round to take his seat Chameleon dropped off and landed on the stool.

The hare saw how he had been tricked and was very angry. The other animals, however, arrived before he could harm the chameleon. According to the agreement they had made, they had no choice but to make chameleon.

But none of the animals were satisfied with the choice. So as soon as the meeting was over, all scattered in every direction and left Chameleon quite alone.

He was so ashamed that he went and made his home at the top of a very high tree on a mountain. In the dead of night you may hear him calling his attendants to come and stay with him. But he is left quite alone. "A king without subjects is no king."

THE FOOLISH SPIDER̄
WHO LOST AN ELEPHANT
FOR A BIRD

IN olden times there stood in the King's town a very great tree. This tree was so huge that it began to overshadow the neighbouring fields. The King decided to have it cut down. He caused his servants to proclaim throughout the country that anyone who succeeded in cutting down the tree with a wooden axe should have an elephant in payment.

People thought it would be impossible to cut down such a great tree with an axe of wood. Spider, however, decided to try by cunning to gain the elephant. He accordingly presented himself before the King and expressed his readiness to get rid of the tree.

A servant was sent with him to keep watch and to see that he only used the wooden axe given him. Spider, however, had taken care to have another, made of steel, hidden in his bag.

He now began to fell the tree. In a very few minutes, he said to the servant, "see, yonder is a fine antelope. If you are quick, you will be able to hit it with a stone. Run! The lad did as he was bid, and ran a long way – but could see no sign of the antelope. In his absence, Spider seized the sharp axe and hastened to cut as much of the tree as he could, carefully hide the axe in his bag before the servant's return.

This trick he repeated several times, till finally the tree was cut down. Spider went to the King to get the elephant, and took the servant to prove that he had used only the wooden axe. He got his promised reward, and started for home in great glee. On the way, however, he began to think over the matter. "Shall I take this animal home?" thought he. "That would be foolish, for then I would be obliged to share it with my family. No! I will hide it in the forest, and eat it at my leisure. In that way I can have the whole of it for myself. Now what can I take home for the children's dinner?"

Thereupon he looked around, and, a little distance, saw a tiny bird sitting on a tree. "Exactly what I want," he said to himself. "That will be quite sufficient for them. I will tie my elephant to this tree while I catch the bird."

This he did, but when he tried to seize the latter, it flew off. He chased it for some time, without success. "Well! Well! Said he. "My family will just have to go without dinner. I will now go back and get my elephant." He returned to the spot where he had left the animal, but to his dismay the latter had escaped. Spider was obliged to go home empty-handed, and him as well as his family, went without dinner that day.

THE UNGRATEFUL MAN

A HUNTER, who was terribly poor, was one day walking through the forest in search of food. Coming to a deep hole, he found there a leopard, a serpent, a rat, and a man. These had all fallen into the trap and were unable to get out again. Seeing the hunter, they begged him to help them out of the hole.

At first he did not wish to release any but the man. The leopard, he said, had often stolen his cattle and eaten them. The serpent very frequently bit men and caused their death. The rat did no good to anyone. He saw no use in setting them free.

However, these animals pleaded so hard for life that at last he helped them out of the pit. Each, in turn, promised to reward him for his kindness – except the man. He, saying he was very poor, was taken home by the kind-hearted hunter and allowed to stay with him.

A short time after, serpent came to the hunter and gave him a very powerful antidote for snake-poison. "Keep it carefully," said serpent. "You will find it very useful one day. When you are using it, be sure to ask for the blood of a traitor to mix with it." The hunter, having thanked serpent very much, took great care of the powder and always carried it about with him.

The leopard also showed his gratitude by killing animals for the hunter and supplying him with food for many weeks.

Then, one day, the rat came to him and gave him a large bundle. "These," said he, "are some native cloths, gold dust, and ivory. They will make you rich." The hunter thanked the rat very heartily and took the bundle into his cottage.

After this the hunter was able to live in great comfort. He built himself a fine new house and supplied it with everything needful. The man whom he had taken out of the pit still lived with him.

This man, however, was of a very envious disposition. He was not at all pleased at his host's good fortune, and only waited an opportunity to do him some harm. He very soon had a chance.

A proclamation was sounded throughout the country to say that some robbers had broken into the King's palace and stolen his jewels and many other valuables. The ungrateful man instantly hurried to the King and asked what the reward would be if he pointed out the thief. The King promised to give him half of the things which had been stolen. The wicked fellow

thereupon falsely accused his host of the theft, although he knew quite well that he was innocent.

The honest hunter was immediately thrown into prison. He was then brought into Court and requested to show how he had become so rich. He told them, faithfully, the source of his income, but no one believed him. He was condemned to die the following day at noon.

Next morning, while preparations were being made for his execution, word was brought to the prison that the King's eldest son had been bitten by a serpent and was dying. Anyone who could cure him was begged to come and do so.

The hunter immediately thought of the powder which his serpent friend had given him, and asked to be followed to use it. At first they were unwilling to let him try, but finally he received permission. The King asked him if there were anything is needed for it and he replied, "A traitor's blood to mix it with." His Majesty immediately pointed out the wicked fellow who had accused the hunter and said: "There stands who the worst traitor – for he gave up the kind host who had saved his life." The man was at once beheaded and the powder was mixed as the serpent commanded. As soon as it was applied to the prince's wound the young man was cured. In great delight, the King loaded the hunter with honours and sent him happily home.

WHY LEOPARDS NEVER ATTACK MEN
UNLESS THEY ARE PROVOKED

A MAN, hunting one day in the forest, met a leopard. At first each was afraid of the other; but after some talking they became quite friendly. They agreed to live together for a little time. First the man would live with the leopard in his forest home for two weeks. Then the leopard would come and live in the man's home.

The leopard behaved so well to the man during his visit that the man felt he had never been so well treated in his life. Then came the time for the leopard to return home with man. As they were going the leopard was somewhat afraid. He asked the man if he really thought he would be safe. "What if your friends do not like my face and kill me?"" he asked. "You need fear nothing," said his host; "no one will touch you while I am there." The leopard therefore came to the man's house and stayed with him for three weeks. He had brought his male cub with him, and the young leopard became friendly with the man's son.

Some months later the man's father died. When Leopard heard of his friend's great loss, he and his cub set out at once to see and condole with him. They brought a large sum of money to help the man.

As leopard was going home again two of the man's friends lay in hiding for him and shot him. Fortunately he was not killed, but he was very much grieved lest these men had shot at his friend's wish. He determined to find out if the man had known anything at all about the shot.

Accordingly he went to the place in the forest where he had first met his friend. There he lay down as if he were dead, after telling his cub to watch and see what would happen.

By and by the man came along. When he saw the leopard lying, as he thought, dead, he was terribly troubled. He began to cry and mourn for his friend, and sat there all night long with Leopard's cub, to watch that no harm should befall the body.

When morning came and Leopard was quite assured that his friend had had nothing at all to do with the shot, he was very glad. He got up, then, to the man's great astonishment, and explained why he had pretended to be dead.

"Go home," said Leopard, "and remember me always. In future for your sake I will never touch a man unless he first meddles with me."

THE OMANHENE̅
WHO LIKED RIDDLES

THE Omanhene is the chief of a village. A certain Omanhene had three sons, who were very anxious to see the world. They went to their father and asked permission to travel. This permission he readily gave.

It was the turn of the eldest to go first. He was provided with a servant and with all he could possibly require for the journey.

After travelling for some time he came to a town where an Omanhene who loved riddles lived. Being a stranger the traveller was, according to custom, brought by the people before the chief.

The latter explained to him that they had certain laws in their village. One law was that every stranger must beat the Omanhene in answering riddles or he would be beheaded. He must be prepared to begin the contest the following morning.

Next day he came to the Assembly Place, and found the Omanhene there with all his attendants. The Omanhene asked many riddles. As the young man was unable to answer any of them, he was judged to have failed and was beheaded.

After some time the second son of the Omanhene started on his travels. By a strange chance he arrived at the same town where his brother had died. He also was asked many riddles, and failed to answer them. Accordingly he too was put to death.

By and by the third brother announced his intention of traveling. His mother did all in her power to persuade him to stay at home. It was quite in vain.

She was sure that if he also reached the town where his brothers had died, the same thing would happen to him. Rather than allow this, she thought she would prefer him to die on the way.

She prepared for him a food called kenke – which she filled with poison. Having packed it away in his bag, he set off. Very soon he began to feel hungry. Knowing, however, that his mother had not wished him to leave home, and therefore might have put some poison in the food, he thought he would test it before eating it himself. Seeing a vulture nearby, he threw it half the cake.

The bird ate the kenke, and immediately fell dead by the roadside. Three leopards came along and began to eat the vulture. They also fell dead.

The young man cut off some of the flesh of the leopards and roasted it. He then packed it carefully away in his bundle.

A little farther on he was attacked by seven highway robbers. They wanted to kill him at once. He told them that he had some good roast meat in his bundle and invited them to eat with him first. They agreed and divided up the food into eight parts.

While they were eating the young man carefully hid his portion. Soon all the seven robbers fell ill and died. The young man went on his way.

At last he reached the town where his brothers had died. Like them, he was summoned to the Assembly Place to answer the riddles of the Omanhene. For two days the contest proved equal. At the end of that time, the young man said, "I have only one riddle left. If you are able to answer that, you may put me to death." He then gave this riddle to the Omanhene:

Half kills one –

One kills three –

Three kills seven.

The ruler failed to answer it that evening, so it was postponed till the next day.

During the night the Omanhene disguised himself and went to the house where the stranger was staying. There he found the young man asleep in the hall.

Imagining that the man before him was the stranger's servant, and never dreaming that it was the stranger himself, he roused the sleeper and promised him a large reward if he would give him the solution to the riddle.

The young man replied that he would tell the answer if the Omanhene would bring him the costume which he always wore at the Assembly.

The ruler was only too pleased to go and fetch it for him. When the young had the garments quite safely, he explained the riddle fully to the crafty Omanhene. He said that as they were leaving home, the mother of his master made him kenke. In order to find out if the kenke were good, they gave half to a vulture. The latter died. Three leopards which tasted the vulture also died. A little of the leopards' roasted flesh killed seven robbers.

The Omanhene was delighted to have found out the answer. He warned the supposed servant not to tell his master what had happened.

In the morning all the villagers assembled together again. The Omanhene proudly gave the answer to the riddle as if he himself had found it out. But the young man asked him to produce his ceremonial dress, which he ought to be wearing in Assembly. This, of course, he was unable to do, as the young man had hidden it carefully away.

The stranger then told what had happened in the night, and how the ruler had got the answer to the riddle by cheating.

The Assembly declared that the Omanhene had failed to find out the riddle and must die. Accordingly he was beheaded – and the young man was appointed Omanhene in his place.

HOW MUSHROOMS FIRST GREW IN THE WORLD

LONG, long ago there dwelt in a town two brothers whose bad habits brought them much trouble. Day by day they got more deeply in debt. Their creditors gave them no peace, so at last they ran away into the woods. They became highways robbers.

But they were not happy. Their minds were troubled by their evil deeds. At last they decided to go home, make a big farm, and pay off their debts gradually.

They accordingly set to work and soon had quite a fine farm prepared for corn. As the soil was good, they hoped the harvest would bring them in much money.

Unfortunately, that very day a bush-fowl came along. Being hungry, it starched up all the newly planted seeds and ate them.

The two poor brothers, on arriving at the field next day, were dismayed to find all their work quite wasted. They put down a trap for the thief. That evening the bush-fowl was caught in it. The two brothers, when they came and found the bird, told it that now all their debts would be transferred to it because it had robbed them of the means of paying the debts themselves.

The poor bird – in great trouble at having such a burden thrust upon it – made a nest under a silk-cotton tree. There it began to lay eggs, meaning to hatch them and sell the young birds for money to pay off the debt.

A terrible hurricane came, however, and a branch of the tree came down. All the eggs were smashed. As a result, the bush fowl transferred the debts to the tree, as it had broken the eggs.

The silk-cotton tree was in dismay at having such a big sum of money to pay off. It immediately set to work to make as much silk cotton as it possibly could, that it might sell it.

An elephant, not knowing all that had happened, came along. Seeing the silk cotton, he came to the tree and plucked down all its bearings. By this means the debts were transferred to the poor elephant.

The elephant was very sad when he found what he has done. He wandered away into the desert, thinking of away to make money. He could think of none.

As he stood quietly under a tree, a poor hunter crept up. This man thought he was very lucky to find such a fine elephant standing so still. He at once shot him.

Just before the animal died, he told the hunter that now the debts would have to be paid by him. The hunter was much grieved when heard this, as he had no money at all.

He walked home wondering what he could do to make enough money to pay the debts. In the darkness he did not see the stump of a tree which the overseers had cut down in the road. He fell and broke his leg. By this means the debts were transferred to the tree-stump.

Not knowing this, a party of white ants came along next morning and began to eat into the tree. When they had broken it nearly to the ground, the tree told them that now the debts were theirs, as they had killed it.

The ants, being very wise, held a council together to find out how best they could make money. They decided each to contribute as much as possible. With the proceeds one of their young men would go to the nearest market and buy pure linen thread. This they would weave and sell and the profits would go to help pay the debts.

This was done. From time to time all the linen in stock was brought and spread out in the sunshine to keep it in good condition. When men see this linen lying out on the ant-hills, the call it 'mushroom,' and gather it for food.

THE FARMER AND
THE HELPFUL SPIRITS

FARMER MAGAVA was one day looking about for a suitable piece of land to convert into a field. He wished to grow corn and yams. He discovered a fine spot, close to a great forest – which latter was the home of some spirits. He set to work at once to prepare the field.

Having sharpened his great knife, he began to cut down the bushes. No sooner had he touched one than he heard a voice say, "Who is there, cutting down the bushes?" Magava was too much astonished to answer. The question was repeated. This time the farmer realized that it must be one of the spirits, and so replied, "I am Magava, come to prepare a field." Fortunately for him the spirits were in great good humour. He heard one say, "Let us all help farmer Magava to cut down the bushes." The rest agreed. To Magava's great delight, the bushes were all rapidly cut down – with very little trouble on his part. He returned home, exceedingly well pleased with his day's work, having resolved to keep the field a secret from his wife.

Early in January, when it was time to burn the dry bush, he set off to his field, on afternoon, with the means of making a fire. Hoping to have the spirits' assistance once more, he intentionally struck the trunk of a tree and he passed. Immediately came the questions, "Who is there, striking the stumps?" He promptly replied, "I am Magava, come to burn down the bush." Accordingly, the dried bushes were all burned down, and the field left clear in less time than it takes to tell it.

Next day the same thing happened. Magava came to chop up the stumps for firewood and clear the field for digging. In a very short time his faggots and firewood were piled ready, while the field was bare.

So it went on. The field was divided into two parts – one for maize and one for yams. In all the preparations – digging, sowing, planting – the spirits gave great assistance. Still, the farmer had managed to keep the whereabouts of his field a secret from his wife and neighbours.

The soil having been so carefully prepared, the crops promised exceedingly well. Magava visited them from time to time, and congratulated himself on the splendid harvest he would have.

One day, while maize and yams were still in their green and milky state, Magava's wife came to him. She wished to know where his field lay, that she might go fetch some of firewood from it. At first he refused to tell her. Being very persistent, however, she finally succeeded in obtaining the information – but on once condition. She must not answer any question that should be asked her. This she readily promised, and set off for the field.

When she arrived there she was utterly amazed at the wealth of the corn and yam. She had never seen such magnificent crops. The maize looked most tempting – being still in the milky state – so she plucked an ear. While doing she heard a voice, "Who is there, breaking the corn?" "Who dares ask me such a question?" she replied angrily – quite forgetting her husband's command. Going to the field of yams she plucked one of them also."Who is there, picking the yams?" came the question again. "It is I, Magava's wife. This is my husband's field and I have a right to pick." Out came the spirits. "Let us all help Magava's wife to pluck her corn and yams," said they. Before the frightened woman would say a word, the spirits had all set to work with a will and the corn and yams lay useless to the ground. Being all green and unripe, the harvest was now utterly spoiled. The farmer's wife wept bitterly, but to no purpose. She returned slowly home, not knowing what to say to her husband about such a terrible catastrophe. She decided to keep silence about the matter.

Accordingly, next day the poor man set off gleefully to his field to see how his fine crops were going on. His anger may be imagined when he saw his field a complete ruin. All his work and foresight had been absolutely ruined through his wife's forgetfulness of her promise.

END